Marion Harland

**Charlotte Brontë at Home**

Marion Harland

**Charlotte Brontë at Home**

ISBN/EAN: 9783337139025

Printed in Europe, USA, Canada, Australia, Japan

Cover: Foto ©Raphael Reischuk / pixelio.de

More available books at **www.hansebooks.com**

# Literary Hearthstones

Studies of the Home-Life of
Certain Writers and Thinkers

# CHARLOTTE BRONTË

CHARLOTTE BRONTË

# CHARLOTTE BRONTË
## AT HOME

BY

MARION HARLAND

AUTHOR OF "SOME COLONIAL HOMESTEADS AND THEIR
STORIES," "WHERE GHOSTS WALK," ETC.

ILLUSTRATED

G. P. PUTNAM'S SONS
NEW YORK AND LONDON
The Knickerbocker Press
1899

The Knickerbocker Press, New York

To

# THE REVEREND J. WADE

FOR THIRTY-SEVEN YEARS INCUMBENT OF HAWORTH

IN CORDIAL APPRECIATION OF THE UNFAILING COURTESY AND
KINDLY AID EXTENDED BY HIM TO THE AMERICAN STRANGER
WITHIN HIS GATES

THIS VOLUME IS

GRATEFULLY DEDICATED

## PREFATORY

THIS simple narrative of the domestic
life of Charlotte Brontë is as careful
and patient as conscience and affection could
make it. When practicable, I verified by
personal investigation what I had heard and
read. When dependent upon information
received from others, I consulted what
seemed to me the ablest authorities upon a
subject which has been treated by many,
with more or less skill.

To no other published work upon the
Brontë family am I so much indebted as to
the most interesting volume lately issued
by Professor Clement K. Shorter under the
title of *Charlotte Brontë and Her Circle.* It
is candid, scholarly, and comprehensive,
and to it my final appeal was made when
other biographers differed as to leading
facts, or were confusing in details. It has
taken its place—and will hold it—as a

standard classic in whatever pertains to the life-story of a great woman.

My grateful acknowledgments are herewith offered to the Reverend J. Wade, late of Haworth Rectory; to Mr. Richard Hewitt of Bradford, England, and to Mrs. Mary N. Stull of Iowa City (Ia.), the faithful amanuensis of her agèd mother, Mrs. Newsome, formerly Sarah De Garrs.

MARION HARLAND.

SUNNYBANK, POMPTON, N. J.

## POST-PREFATORY

AFTER the first edition of this biography was printed, I received the news of the death of Mrs. Newsome (Sarah De Garrs), the nursery governess and friend of the Brontë children, and of whom frequent mention is made in the story of Charlotte's life.

Mrs. Newsome died in Iowa City, September 9, 1899, at the great age of ninety-three years and thirteen days. She preserved her mental powers to a marvellous degree, up to the last day of her life, passing away as peacefully as she had lived.

The mail that brought me intelligence of her decease placed in my hands a copy of the following interesting letter from Mr. Brontë to Mrs. Newsome. It is valuable as indicating the friendly relations existing between the two, and it is creditable to

the hearts of both. I regret exceedingly
that it did not reach me in season to be
wrought into the body of my narrative.

MARION HARLAND.

*July 12, 1855.*

MRS. SARAH NEWSOME,

    CRAWFORDSVILLE, IOWA, U. S. A.

*Dear Mrs. Newsome :*—I have duly received your
kind letter and am glad to learn from it that you and
your husband and family are well and doing well in the
new world. May God bless and protect you all, both
in things spiritual and temporal!

Since you were with me many solemn and important
changes have taken place in my domestic affairs.
When you and your sister Nancy first came to us at
Thornton, my dear children were living, seven in number. They are dead, and I, hovering on the age of
eighty years, am left alone. But it is God's will to do
this, and it is our duty and wisdom to resign.

You probably little thought that the children you
nursed on your knees would be as much noticed by the
world as they have been. Emily and Annie wrote and
published clever books, and Charlotte's writings and
fame are known in all parts of the world where genius
and learning are held in due estimation. My dear
daughter Charlotte was the last child I had living. She
married the Rev. Arthur Bell Nicholls, a very worthy
and respectable clergyman, and their union was happy
as long as it lasted, but at the end of nine months this
happy union was dissolved by my daughter's death.

Her loving husband and I are left to mourn her irreparable loss.   She died childless.

Your sister Nancy was here a few months since, and from her we learned that your family were all well. The weather here is favourable, crops are promising, and trade on the improvement.   I am glad America, in these respects, is in a prosperous condition.   My children and I often thought and talked of you.   Write a few lines to let me know whether you have duly received this letter.   I remain,

Your Sincere Friend,

P. BRONTË.

INCUMBENT OF HAWORTH, YORKSHIRE.

# CONTENTS

# ILLUSTRATIONS

# CHARLOTTE BRONTË AT HOME

## CHAPTER I

### BIRTH AT THORNTON—REMOVAL TO HAWORTH

"OUR England is a bonnie island, and Yorkshire is one of her bonniest nooks."

The sentence is put by Charlotte Brontë into the mouth of Shirley, the piquante heroine of the novel bearing that name.

The country town of Thornton in the county of Yorkshire could not have been in the writer's mind when she wrote the encomium. It straggles vaguely over wind-swept hills, green in summer, but from which the bleakness associated with tree-less sides and gloomy brows never departs.

The best of the houses are mere cottages, many little better than peasants' cabins; all are of stone, quarried from neighbouring hills, and stained black by fogs and rains.

In the days antedating railways, Thornton was a large hamlet, one third the size of the present place. A thin line of houses extended to what was known as the "Old Denholme Road." This cut at right angles the broader and more level highway to the manufacturing city of Bradford. Other steep cross streets have laid themselves out parallel with the Denholme Road, and are, even now, adorned on washing-day with lines of wet clothes, stretched quite across the thoroughfare [?] from opposite second-storey windows. The heavy-laden ropes droop so low that no vehicles, except hand-barrows, can pass beneath. The universality of the custom argues neighbourly good-will, a spirit of accommodation to circumstances, and generous faith in the amiability of carters and cabmen, who never interfere with the routine of domestic duties. Loud-voiced, bare-armed women, their petticoats kilted high above bare or broganed feet, clack socially together while hanging out the dripping linen, and rail in unison at children playing hide-and-seek among the flapping "wash."

Dante speaks of an old man whom Death had forgotten to strike. Progress has over-looked this one of Yorkshire's nooks. The whistle of the locomotive tearing onward, between the inhospitable hills, to Bradford and Leeds, dies into shrill sighs in valleys dotted with the everlasting stone cottages. Here and there, in a defile, or upon an easy slope, towers a tall factory chimney, belch-ing pitchy smoke, hanging low for nine months of the year, and showering down sooty flakes to heighten the sepia effect of the monotoned landscape.

In 1816, the Rev. Patrick Brontë, late Curate of Hartshead, a Yorkshire living near Huddersfield, removed to Thornton with his wife and two infant children. He was the son of an Irish farmer and the only one of the family who received a liberal education. The name, originally O'Prunty, was registered in Cambridge by the am-bitious lad as Branty. By the time he had taken orders and entered upon his first curacy in Weatherfield, Essex, he wrote it Brontë.

"To me it is perfectly clear," decides Mr. Clement

K. Shorter, "that, for the change of name Lord Nelson was responsible, and that the dukedom of Brontë, which was conferred upon the great sailor in 1799, suggested the more ornamental surname. There were no Irish Brontës in existence before Nelson became Duke of Brontë."

As a handsome young curate, with plenty to say for himself, and a graphic way of saying it, Mr. Brontë had acquired a reputation for gallantry and susceptibility to the charms of the other sex before he put his last crop of wild oats into the ground, in 1812, by marrying Maria Branwell, a pretty, delicate girl from Penzance, in Cornwall. The two met and fell in love while Miss Branwell was on a visit to a Yorkshire uncle. The marriage took place December 18, 1812. Each had attained the conventional age of discretion, Maria Branwell being twenty-eight, Patrick Brontë thirty-three years old.

The house in which they lived in Thornton still stands upon the principal business street of that village. It is two-storeyed. Half of what was then the front yard is covered by a sort of butcher's booth, hardly worthy of the name of shop, set flush with the sidewalk. Passing through this we enter a fair-sized chamber, lighted by a

single window overlooking the small garden
at the back. A corresponding front window
was closed by the shop. Naked rafters
cross the ceiling, in bold relief. The small
grate in the chimney is the same that took
the chill off the spring air, April 21, 1816,
when Charlotte, the Brontës' third daughter, was born in the ground-floor chamber.
There are two other rooms on this floor.
A small kitchen is at the back ; out of it
the stairs run directly to the upper storey.
A parlour, of the same size as Mrs. Brontë's
bedroom, adjoins it. Above-stairs are two
chambers of unequal dimensions. That
over the parlour was Mr. Brontë's study,
and, although in order to reach it he had
to pass through the one spare-chamber in
the humble establishment, he was comparatively secluded from the wailings and
rompings of the three babies below. Nursery there was none, and the parlour, in
which the family took their meals, was
also the sitting-room.

Small as the place is, and unpretending
as was the style of living in the retired hamlet, housewifely tasks and the care of the
trio of children—the eldest, Maria, being
but three years old when Charlotte was

born—must have been a cruel tax upon the mother's strength. She had been brought up in the gentler climate of the southern coast of England—"where plants which we in the north call greenhouse flowers, grow in great profusion, and without any shelter even in winter, and where the soft, warm air allows the inhabitants to live pretty constantly in the open air." Her associates there were her kith and kin and neighbours whom she had known all her life, people of a totally different order from the small shopkeepers, mechanics, and peasants who composed her husband's cure of souls.

"Her mind," said her daughter Charlotte in 1850, "was of a truly fine, pure, and elevated order." And of the letters written by Maria Branwell to her lover during the brief season of their betrothal,—"There is a rectitude, a refinement, a constancy, a modesty, a sense, a gentleness about them, indescribable. I wish she had lived, and that I had known her!"

"I am certain," writes Maria to her betrothed, less than a fortnight before the wedding-day, "no one ever loved you with an affection more pure, constant,

HOUSE IN THORNTON IN WHICH CHARLOTTE BRONTË
WAS BORN

tender and ardent than that which I feel.
I long to improve in every religious and
moral quality that I may be a help, and, if
possible, an ornament to you." *

Untold myriads of other brides have
thus dreamed, and aspired, and awakened
to the stern realism of every-day married
life, many with a shock that expelled love
with hope. Mrs. Brontë must have dismissed the dear desire of being an ornament
to her husband before she lay down, for
the third time in four years, upon her couch
of pain, and brought another weakling girl
into the world.

Baby Charlotte was two months old
when she was presented for baptism (June
29, 1816) at the font in the Thornton Church.
The building, now a picturesque ruin, is
more interesting to the thoughtful visitor
than the shabby-genteel house in which
Charlotte Brontë was born. The frame of
one fine window is intact in the gable,
which is all that remains of the sacred edifice beyond the foundations, a crumbling
wall a few feet high, and some memorial-
slabs that once floored the chancel. Until
very lately the font, which appears in our

* Shorter's *Charlotte Brontë and Her Circle*, page 51.

illustration, was left where it stood when
the baby was baptised by her father's friend
and her mother's cousin-in-law, the Rev.
William Morgan of Bradford.   Mr. Morgan
and Jane Fennell were married on the
same day and hour with Mr. Brontë and
Maria Branwell, Mr. Brontë performing the
ceremony for Miss Fennell and Mr. Morgan,
the latter clergyman returning the favour
by uniting his wife's cousin to Patrick
Brontë.   We like to believe that the near
neighbourhood of her cousin—but four miles
distant by the coach-road—tempered, in
some degree, the asperities of life to the
fragile little mistress of Thornton Parsonage.   We choose to imagine, also, that
Jane Fennell may have been in church
on June 29,—perhaps in the capacity of
godmother.

The ruined church and its smarter successor across the road—to which the weather-
beaten font has been removed—are a full
mile from the Parsonage by way of the
winding highways I have described.   As
the Brontës never kept a carriage, the
oft-ailing mother would be an infrequent
attendant upon her robust husband's min-
istrations.   Yet her feet must sometimes

have pressed the hoary stones we part
coarse wild grasses to trace, and the
graceful outlines of the window behind
the altar were familiar to meek eyes which
rested upon little else that was beautiful or
inspiring. The churchyard she crossed to
reach the house of prayer, and through
which the Reverend Patrick strode twice
a week during the four years of his Thornton incumbency, is overgrown with grass,
weeds, and such hardy garden-plants as
southernwood, lavender, and rosemary. In
June, pinks bloom in the crevices of neg-
lected tombs, and English ivy—kindliest
of creepers—drapes the broken walls of
the church. Under the very droppings of
the sanctuary-eaves was buried, over a
century ago, one whose story is thus told:

*" Here lyeth the Body of Mr. Accepted
Lister, Minister of the Gospel, who exchanged this Frail Life for a Better, February the 25, 178/9, Anno Ætatis 38. He had,
by his abundant Labours, verified his own
Motto,—*

*" ' Impendam et Expendar.' "*

Mr. Brontë was ever a valiant Church-
man. We hope, charitably, that when

called upon to read the Burial Service over some one of the numerous "family graves" that are thick on that side of the church, his falcon gaze rested respectfully, not in scorn, upon the epitaph of the Puritan Non-Conformist who wore out his frail body at thirty-eight in the strenuous endeavour to live up to his "Motto."

One year and less than a month after Charlotte's christening, Mrs. Brontë's uncle, Rev. John Fennell, baptised in Thornton Church the only son ever born to Patrick Brontë and Maria, his wife.  The child received his father's Christian name and the surname of his mother's family, and became, as Patrick Branwell, the most important personage of the household in his parents' estimation, afterward, and always in his own.

Charlotte's one distinct recollection of her mother, in after-years, was of a pale little lady playing with her two-year-old son in the fire-lighted Haworth parlour, one wintry evening.  There was no reason why the picture should have stamped itself upon the childish mind, unless it were that the occasions were pitifully rare when the mother had time or spirits for frolicking, even with her idolised boy.

RUINS OF BELL CHAPEL IN THORNTON

The friendly kinsman, Rev. William Morgan, came to the front again, August 20, 1818, the Sunday on which the Brontës' fifth child and fourth daughter received the name of Emily Jane, in affectionate remembrance of Mrs. Morgan, the sister-cousin of Maria Branwell's girlhood.

By now, it was a matter of course that the Parson should have a new baby every year to show to the rural congregation. The Register of Baptisms in the Parish of Bradford and Chapelry of Thornton contains two entries that deviate from the four-year-old record. Anne Brontë was not offered for baptism until March 25, 1820, and her father is set down, not as " Minister of Thornton," as at Charlotte's christening, or, as when Emily's turn came, "of Thornton Parsonage," but as " Minister of Haworth." He had been appointed to the living of that place a month or so prior to Anne's birth.

Mrs. Gaskell thinks the family removal to Haworth took place in February, 1820. In that case, the baby would hardly have been christened in Thornton a month later. Mrs. Brontë, never strong, was a confirmed invalid after Anne's birth, and the

four-mile drive over the hills would have
been needless exposure for mother and
child at that inclement season.   It was
probably later in the spring that comes
coyly, and never early, to that region, that
seven country carts, laden with books,
household and kitchen furniture, creaked
through the one long street of Old Haworth,
the horses tugging uphill all the way, to
the gate of the Parsonage.

Mrs. Gaskell "wonders how the bleak
aspect of her new home—the low, oblong
stone Parsonage, high up, with a still
higher background of sweeping moors—
struck on the gentle, delicate wife."

The impression would have been more
painful but for the middle age of her residence in Thornton.   The wildness of the
latter hamlet was less forbidding than Haworth at that time of the year; still, the
general features of village and country were
the same.   The vast moors, stretching out
on all sides and upward, beyond the last
row of stone cottages and the group of
church buildings, were more open to the
searching winds of the North Country than
the inferior heights about Thornton.   The
winters might be longer here, and the fogs

rising from the deeper hollows, heavier.
The Parsonage itself, cheerless though it is
to our eyes, was a decided improvement in
size and convenience upon the cramped
quarters on the business street which Mrs.
Brontë left behind her, while Haworth
Church, venerable in antiquity and in tradition, represented a better living than the Bell
Chapel of Thornton. The grey old sanctuary, separated by a churchyard as ancient
from the Brontës' new home, occupied a
site consecrated and used as an oratory in
the fourteenth century; the parish was
larger and richer than either of the other
livings Mr. Brontë had held, and was rated
as a desirable position by the rural clergy.

It may, then, have been with a lighter,
not a heavier, spirit that the mother entered
her new abode, and gathered her six babies
about the hearthstone in the parlour—the
parlour that was to be the living-room of
the family for the rest of their mortal lives,
and the birth-chamber of the immortal
books which have made it a shrine to a
million pilgrims.

# CHAPTER II

## THE SIX BABIES IN HAWORTH PARSONAGE

HAWORTH PARSONAGE, as all the reading world knows, stands upon higher ground than the church. A tiny door-yard is in front, divided from the burying-ground by a brick wall. Behind are fields sloping upward to the rolling moors. The graveyard lies upon the front and one end of the dwelling, and, on the upper gable-end, is higher than the house grounds, suggesting gruesome thoughts as to the quality of the water drained into the well for cooking and drinking purposes. There are four rooms upon the first floor, with a central hall. The apartment at the right of the front door was assigned at once to Mr. Brontë as a study. Back of it, but with no communicating door, was the kitchen. It had one window, and a rear door giving

upon the yard.  Opposite the study was
the parlour.  This was the family eating-
room, and they had no other place in
which to receive visitors.  Next to this,
and across the hall from the kitchen, was a
storeroom.  Mr. Brontë's bedchamber was
directly above the study, and as declining
health soon compelled his wife to have a
separate sleeping-room, she took that over
the parlour.  A servants' dormitory above
the storeroom could be warmed by a
grate, if necessary.  The nursery was cut
off from the upper front hall.  The solitary
window looked upon the graveyard and
the church.  There was neither fireplace nor
stove in it.  The winter's chill and the spring
dampness must have got into the stone wall
and flagged flooring, and lingered there
until July suns baked the house to its heart.

That was not a luxurious age, and the
children were Yorkshire-born, yet we cannot hear without a shudder that the six
little things had no other playroom than
this ; that they spent hours of every day,
and most of every stormy day here, busy
with their books and the games invented
by themselves.  They had no toys, and no
playfellows outside of the Parsonage.

Mrs. Brontë brought to Haworth a young
girl of fourteen or thereabouts, Sarah De
Garrs by name, the daughter of a respectable Thornton parishioner, to assist in the
nursery and to accompany the children in
their walks. Although nominally their
nurse, she became at length their play-
mate, friend, and guardian. Mrs. Brontë
sickened visibly that first summer in the
new home, and by the time winter closed
about the moorland Parsonage, was confined to her bed, unable to take the over-
sight of the household, seeing the children
but twice a day, and then for a few
minutes only.

Maria (the original of Helen Burns in
*Jane Eyre*) was now seven, and the "little
mother" of the band. Her father had taught
her to read, and to think. There were no
juvenile books in his library. He would
have proscribed them if there had been
any. Even after Sarah De Garrs's sister
Nancy was associated with her in the conduct of the house, the work was too heavy
to permit the attached nurse to devote
much time to amusing the children. There
was no longer any attempt to disguise the
fatal truth that Mrs. Brontë's malady was

an internal cancer. The seed of the evil was in the scrofulous humour which developed with deadly effect in her offspring. It matters not now how much annual child-bearing, a sour and sharp climate, overwork, and narrow means had to do with hasten-ing the end. She lay in bed all day, suffer-ing intense pain at times, and so miserably unnerved that the house must be kept perfectly quiet when she "had her worst turns."

I have had direct from Sarah De Garrs * the story of one day in the overshadowed home, a routine laid down and carried out by the father—for all these months sick-nurse, tutor, breadwinner, and bread-dis-penser to the little flock already virtually motherless.

The six children, always neatly dressed by their nurse, met their father in his study for morning prayers, and, these over, ac-companied him across the hall to breakfast. The fare was plain, but abundant,—porridge and milk, bread and butter, for the morning meal seven days in the week. The furni-ture of the parlour was scanty, yet well kept. The grate was economically contrived

* *Now Mrs. Newsome of Iowa City.*

to burn the least quantity of coals consistent
with enough warmth to save the occupants
of the room from actual suffering; there
were two small windows, both looking
toward the burial-ground.   Mr. Brontë
discouraged table-talk,—for a while, lest the
clamour of tongues might break the quiet
of the sick-room overhead ; after Mrs.
Brontë's death, because his digestion had
been damaged seriously by night-watching
and irregular meals snatched in the intervals of trying offices there was nobody but
the husband to perform.

"He was very attentive and affectionate
to his invalid wife," Mrs. Newsome as-
severates, once and again.  "I am certain
she had no *fear*—as many would construe
the word—of her husband.   Only a loving
wife's fear of offending him."

"He was not naturally fond of children,"
Mrs. Gaskell remarks in this connection,
"and felt their frequent appearance on the
scene as a drag, both on his wife's strength,
and as an interruption to the comfort of
the household."

He deserved, then, the more credit for
the systematic, and, in the main, the wise
ordering of their daily living when they

were thus committed entirely to his care. Maria, Elizabeth, Charlotte, Branwell, and Emily followed him to the study after breakfast, Baby Anne remaining with the nurse.

Mr. Brontë was a scholarly man, with fine literary tastes, himself the author of several books, none of which attracted much attention when published. All of them have long been out of print. A volume of *Cottage Poems* and *The Rural Minstrel* were written before his marriage; two religious novels, some pamphlets upon churchly themes, and a couple of sermons, afterward.

"Many a prolific writer of the day passes muster as a genius among his contemporaries upon as small a talent," says Mr. Shorter, "and Mr. Brontë does not seem to have given himself any airs as an author."

It is doubtful if he ever spoke of the short-lived publications to his children. The education of his home-class was begun and continued along lines of his own devising, and was, like most of his ideas, original in conception and vigorous in practice. Maria, at seven, read political leaders aloud to her father, discussed politics with him in his study, and expounded them at length to her juniors, when in any other nursery in Christendom they would have been lisping *Three Little Pigs Went to Market,* and making round, pitiful eyes over *The Babes in the Wood.* For text-books the pupils had such manuals and helps to learning as the father had used in preparing himself for Cambridge, supplemented by his inexhaustible memory.

The morning session over, the children were committed to Sarah De Garrs until dinner-time. To her patient tutelage the girls owed much of the skill with the needle which was remarkable with each at a very tender age. At five, Charlotte's wee fingers made a linen chemise for her own wear, with no other help than the cutting and basting done by Sarah.

"Of course," relates the whilom nurse, "she had been a long while at it, as they only sewed an hour each afternoon. But it was clean and well done. Charlotte was always a thoughtful, neat, womanly child."

When the chemise was finished, and the basting-threads withdrawn, Sarah led the little seamstress into her mother's chamber to exhibit her handiwork.

The suggested scene is interesting, and

falls in well with the scheme of Charlotte
Brontë's unique life-history. She was always small for her age, quiet in speech,
and noiseless in her motions, reminding be-
holders of a timid, bright-eyed bird. In
" Mamma's room " she would glide like a
shadow, and have to stand on tiptoe to
hold up the small garment for the bed-
ridden judge's inspection.

When comparatively free from pain, Mrs.
Brontë found entertainment in all that went
on within the strait confines of her prison,
asking her nurse to raise her among the
pillows that she might see the grate polished, " as it used to be done in Cornwall,"
—in the far-off Penzance she had never seen
since she left its bland airs and perpetual
flowering for the eventful visit to the John
Fennells in 1812.

She would be sure to magnify Charlotte's
visit and achievement into an event, taking
the scrap of linen in her wasted hands,
and feigning critical examination of seam,
and gusset, and band. Then would follow
words of praise in the weak voice that
never lost its sweet southern intonations,
and the kiss that fully rewarded the little
one for the " long while" the task was in

doing, and the pains it had cost her to keep it clean.

The children dined with their father. Little meat was served to them, and that little was plain roast or boiled. Mr. Brontë's Irish prejudices and habits inclined him to restrict their diet almost entirely to potatoes and milk for the noon meal. For sweets there were bread- and rice-puddings, custards, and other preparations of eggs and milk, slightly sweetened. Pastry and rich puddings were unknown quantities in the family bill-of-fare.

The afternoons spent by Mr. Brontë in parish visiting were the children's happiest seasons. Unless the weather were actually tempestuous, they donned hats and coats and took the uphill path to the breezy downs, accompanied by Sarah De Garrs.

"My sister Emily loved the moors," wrote Charlotte in her womanhood. "Flowers brighter than the rose bloomed in the blackest of the heath for her. Out of a sullen hollow in a livid hillside, her mind could make an Eden."

For "Emily," read "the Brontë children." The sweep and wide reaches of the uncultivated tracts billowing against the sky,

the clouds that made the heath black, the
sunlight that glorified the livid hillsides,
—were their universe. Once beyond the
Parsonage fields and environing cottages,
their repressed spirits broke forth.

"Their afternoon walks, as they sallied
forth, each neatly and comfortably clad,
were a joy. Their fun knew no bounds,"
says the affectionate nurse. "It never was .
expressed wildly. Bright and often dry,
but deep, it occasioned many a merry burst
of laughter. They enjoyed a game of
romps, and played with zest."

They knew every bird by sight and
name, and the *habitat* and properties of
every plant growing wild in their belovèd
solitudes. The change of seasons was
reckoned by the budding, the blooming,
and the blighting of the heather. The
passionate love of Nature, in her sombre,
and in her blithe moods, that makes Charlotte's slightest descriptive sketch of moon-
rise, or sunset, or rain-storm perfect in
drawing and in colour, was fostered by
face-to-face communion with the Mighty
Mother.

Strolling reluctantly homeward as prudent Sarah detected the creeping of evening

shadows and chill from the valleys, they found tea awaiting them, in the kitchen, if the weather were cold, in the long summer evenings, in the parlour. Mr. Brontë came in later and tea was served in his study. He assembled the children about the table in the parlour when the tea-tray was taken off, for recitation and talk, giving them oral lessons in history, biography, or travel, while the little girls plied their needles. The story told in the evening was to be written down, or repeated to him as part of the morrow's lesson.

The uneventful day was closed by a short visit to their mother's room. While she could listen to them, the little ones said their nightly prayers at her bedside, kissed her "good-night," and stole away softly to "warm, clean beds," as Sarah De Garrs is careful to specify.

To the close of his long life, Mr. Brontë was more the soldier than the divine. He carried his martinet system of work and recreation into the minutest detail of parish and family duties. Method, law, obedience, were his watchwords. It was an age of educational "fads." *La Nouvelle Heloïse* and English *Sandford and Merton* had put new ideas into the minds of parents and instructors. With the Vicar of Haworth idea leaped into action at birth. The word "heredity" had not been coined then, but he had a certain belief in blood, and in the influence of descent upon the growing child. He believed, with all his rugged strength, in environment, and he made it for his young family. Walls of impassable reserve were raised between them and the people of their own caste within a radius of twenty miles who might, otherwise, have made overtures of sociability to the Parsonage.

Mrs. Brontë's ill-health sufficed, while she lived, to excuse the lack of neighbour-liness. By the time she died the household habits were fixed; the father's views began to be comprehended, and, I need not say, to be resented. The sort of Swiss Family Robinson colony set up in the old grey house at the top of the churchyard was an obnoxious novelty to Yorkshire squire and dame. It was less tolerable to their notions of congruity and civility because artisans and day-labourers approved of "a parson who minded his own business and did n't meddle with theirs," and his children were trained to speak politely and kindly to their humble neighbours when they chanced to meet them.

Nothing surprised me more in my intercourse with those of Mr. Brontë's cottage parishioners who recollect him well, than the genuine liking for him expressed by them all. Grey-headed Saturday night loungers in the "Black Bull" tap-room vie with one another in relating stories of his "jolly ways" and his freedom from offensive pride. How he stopped on his way to church to laugh at a fight his dog got into with a vicious tramp cur, and "wor main sorry he cud na' stay to see it oot. He wor sure his dawg wad get the best o't." How he could call by name everybody he met in his long tramps over hill and dale, if he or she were his parishioner, and never forgot to ask after ailing wife or child. How he would walk fifteen miles in the teeth of snow or sleet, to "get himself into a glow-loike," and "care nought for his wet coat and frozen breeches." All agree that "the family kep' theirselves verra close. As indeed they had a roight to do, if they loiked."

Sarah De Garrs's emphatic declaration that "Mr. Brontë was at all times a *gen-*

*tleman*, never showing temper in the least, tender in the sick-room and kind to his children "—confirms the impressions gained from tap-room and cottage gossip, to wit, that the popular verdict upon the eccentric recluse (in which I had heretofore heartily acquiesced) may have been one-sided and unjust.

"He never gave me an angry word !" is one of the three recorded sayings of his devoted wife.

Her love and his daughter's steadfast filial piety may have had more warrant in his character and behaviour than the majority of the Brontë cult are ready to admit.

# CHAPTER III

MRS. BRONTË'S DEATH—MISS BRANWELL—
CHILDREN'S HOME EDUCATION

CHARLOTTE BRONTË was but five years old when the six children were led, in solemn ceremony, to their mother's room to see her die.

The day was September 15, 1821. The weary agony of the cureless malady had lasted a year and a half. Yet enough vitality remained in the emaciated frame to make death a struggle. So hard was it that, as an eye-witness told me, the knees were drawn up rigidly against the body, and could not be straightened when life was extinct.

She had expressed the wish to her husband that "all the dear faces should be about her when she died," and the faithful Sarah carried Baby Anne in her arms when the summons came.   The husband did not leave his post at his wife's pillow until, as he has inscribed upon her memorial-stone, "Her soul departed to her Saviour."

Less aptly he added,—"*Be ye also ready, for, in such an hour as ye think not, the Son of Man cometh.*"

The long-suffering invalid, "always patient, cheerful, and pious," had been not only ready, but expectant of the summons for many a sleepless night and tortured day.

The poor body—so wasted that the wonder was how it had continued to hold the heroic soul thus long—was laid away under the pavement of the church.   Mr. Brontë, reticent of sorrow as of all other deep emotions, readjusted the domestic machinery to move on as if jar and wrench had not been.   Except that the little girls thereafter slept in the room over the parlour, their lives were little changed on the surface.   To all but the deep-hearted Maria,—who had borne a most unchildlike part in the labours and cares that devolved upon the mistress of the fast-growing family,—the mother, when alive, was a shadowy figure, seen seldom, and then under such restraint of youthful spirits as cast a mysterious awe about the large upper chamber and its occupant. She was soon a shadowy memory to Charlotte and the other younger children.

In the pacquet of letters—nine in all—written by her during her betrothal, preserved by the widower, and never showed, even to her children, for a score of years after her decease, was an undated MS. entitled *The Advantages of Poverty in Religious Concerns.* Upon the cover Mr. Brontë had written:

*" The above was written by my dear wife, and is for insertion in one of the religious periodicals. Keep it as a memorial of her."*

We should like to know whether or not the article was ever offered to any of the aforesaid religious periodicals, and why it was not printed. We are yet more interested in asking when the essay was penned. Was it at Hartshead, while the young wife hugged the hope of being an ornament to her husband ? or at Thornton, between the births that turned the slim family purse inside out ? or in intervals separating one pain-paroxysm from the next, in the consecrated "upper chamber" at Haworth ?

Who was the baby in the cradle beside her, as she pursued a theme she should have known by heart, if ever author learned philosophy from experience ?

One day in the autumn or winter succeeding Mrs. Brontë's death, Charlotte came to her nurse, wild and white with the excitement of having seen "a fairy" standing by Baby Anne's cradle.  When the two ran back to the nursery, Charlotte flying on ahead, treading softly not to frighten the beautiful visitant away, no one was there besides the baby sleeping sweetly in the depths of her forenoon nap.  Charlotte stood transfixed ; her eyes wandered incredulously around the room.

"But she *was* here, just now !" she insisted.  "I really and truly did see her !" —and no argument or coaxing could shake her from the belief.

In excluding his children from the world of people and facts, Mr. Brontë drove the eager minds into the universe of imagination.  When they read or listened to a story, they forthwith proceeded to act it. Their "games" were founded upon what Maria read to them from the newspapers, and the tales brought forth from the father's mines of tradition, history, and romance. Nothing escaped them.  Startling melo-dramas and three-volume tales were con-structed upon advertisements in the *Leeds Mercury*, or a "Personal" in a stray copy of the *Times*.

It is pleasant to find their young nurse cast for important parts in these plays.  I copy, from a MS. dictated by her, the ac-count of a *contretemps* that interrupted the orderly progress of scenic adventure :

"As an escaping Prince, with a counterpane for a robe, I stepped from a window on the limb of a cherry-tree, which broke and let me down.  There was great consternation among the children, as it was Mr. Brontë's favourite tree, under which he often sat. I carried off the branch and blackened the place with soot, but the next day, Mr. Brontë detained them a moment and began with the youngest, asking each pleasantly, 'Who spoiled my tree?'  The answer was, 'Not I,' until it came to my turn.  They were always loyal and true."

Apropos of Anne's cradle and Charlotte's attachment to her nurse, is an anecdote of her petition to her father, when Anne had outgrown the little bed, that it should be sent to Sarah's mother, whose baby " would just fit it."  The request was granted, and the story is gratefully recollected by the family who received the gift.

So passed an uneventful year. The course of daily duty and recreation was like clockwork,—prayers, breakfast, lessons in the study, the early dinner, the walks on the moors, the nurse guiding the baby's steps, and lifting Patrick and Emily over rough places; tea in the clean, roomy kitchen; sewing and the informal historical lecture until bedtime. Of this twelve-month—her last in the Parsonage—the agèd nurse says, with a savour of loving jealousy, passing pathetic:

"Their lives were not narrow. They had the nicest system in all that they did, and were a very reserved family, but they found much enjoyment where others could see none. They were *very* happy."

Maria was eight on the 16th of May, 1821, when she "finished her Sampler." Elizabeth finished hers "at the age of seven years," on the 27th of July. Did the fading woman, on whose bed they were laid for inspection as Charlotte's chemise had been, tell each girl of the more elaborate performance in cross-stitch, "ended" April 15, 1791, by Maria Branwell, lettered, thread by thread, with a text she—sweet soul !—

3

surely had then, nor ever, occasion to heed
as an admonition?

*" Flee from sin as from a serpent, for if
thou comest too near to it, it will bite thee.
The teeth thereof are as the teeth of a lion
to slay the souls of men."*

On rainy days,—and they are many in the
Yorkshire uplands,—and when " Papa was
studying," the "little mother" still gathered
her brood in the room overlooking churchyard and church tower, and read to them
by the hour in the subdued tones learned
in the months when a sudden laugh
or incautious exclamation might disturb
" Mamma" next door. Not one of the
girls had a doll! They enacted wars,
and prison-scenes, and heroic adventures
of prince and knight, and fairy-tales—but
they never "played ladies," or had dolls'
tea-parties, or " went visiting" to different
corners of the small room ("the children's
study," as the De Garrs sisters named it),
bedecked with table-covers for cashmere
shawls, and feather-dusters for ostrich-
plumes; never drove a team of chairs lashed
together, or rode horseback sitting sideways on the balustrade. What wonder
that they grew up at once demure and un-

conventional, prim and lawless, shy and daring ?

We are not told if it were kind busybody, or a stirring of worldly wisdom in his own independent spirit, that suggested to Mr. Brontë the need of other society for his motherless girls than that of paid employees, however intelligent and affectionate. The average widower, thus situated, seeks to secure fitting associations and guiding care for the young creatures by a second marriage. Mr. Brontë, loving his liberty and his children, sent to Penzance for his sister-in-law, Miss Elizabeth Branwell, for whom his wife had named their second daughter.

Miss Branwell was middle-aged; she was provincial. Her prejudices, which were many, had rooted themselves stubbornly in forty-five years' residence in one place, and that a country town. The change from the southlands to the bleak, hilly village was a formidable plunge for one of her sex and age. Penzance was always home, Haworth a foreign country. In her rounds of the house whose walls and floors were of stone, and where icy draughts stole in through cracks in the badly fitting window-

and door-frames, the prudent spinster wrapped a shawl about ears and shoulders and shod her feet with iron pattens, the click of which set her nieces' teeth on edge. Their father might ignore, or misapprehend, the protest against Yorkshire barbarities. They loved their country and their home too ardently not to feel the significance of shiver, and shawl, and foot-gear. Whatever dreams they may have indulged, before her advent, of motherly love and sympathy, such as they had never tasted except in brief and tantalising sips, they were speedily dissipated by their aunt's talk and deportment.

Mrs. Brontë, although the youngest, by several years, of four sisters, was looked up to by her family as the most promising member of the Branwell connection. She intimated this modestly to her lover, prior to their marriage, regretting "the disadvantage of having been for some years perfectly her own mistress," and saying how deeply she had "felt the want of a guide and instructor." Her kinspeople regarded her as " possessing more than ordinary talents, which she inherited from her father." Miss Branwell was sensible,

commonplace, and practical in the extreme,
without an atom of intellectuality. Judged
by Cornish standards—and she had at fifty
no other—the condition of her brother-in-
law's home was enough to raise the grey-
ing hair under her cap with dismay. She
and Mr. Brontë seem to have hit it off re-
markably well for two people of utterly
dissimilar training, tastes, and habits, each
of whom was irrevocably addicted to his
and her own opinions. She had the true
middle-class Briton's reverence for his profession, and the British spinsterly respect
for masculinity in the abstract. We hear
of no altercations; each seems to have valued the good qualities of the other; the
widower was profoundly appreciative of
Miss Branwell's notable housewifery and
her honest desire to do her best for his un-
mothered offspring, and his name stood
first among the executors of the will drawn
up by her when she had been an inmate of
the Parsonage for ten years.

The four elder girls were an enigma to
her. They were bashful, they were awkward, they lived in their books, and their
bookish talk was affected gibberish to her.
They had no society and wanted none;

they cared nothing for becoming clothes. Maria was untidy, and Emily had the eyes of a half-tamed creature of another race than the decorous Branwells. All that was most womanly in the newcomer gathered about Anne—"the sweet, loving baby" of Sarah De Garrs's reminiscences. From the beginning she was the aunt's favourite, and, by virtue of his handsome face, his sex, and winning ways, Branwell came next.

The new manager forthwith reorganised the domestic staff, and, with wise thrift, cut down expenses wherever it was practicable. Her activity in this direction had something to do with Mrs. Gaskell's allusion in the *Life of Charlotte Brontë* to "wasteful young servants," a charge refuted by Mr. Brontë's testimonial to their kindness to his children, their honesty and carefulness "in regard to food and all other articles committed to their charge."

Miss Branwell's chamber was a sort of industrial schoolroom where the four elder girls were trained in every description of plain sewing, darning, and knitting. They had their apprenticeship also in the kitchen that was a model of neatness and order for every other in the county. From peeling the potatoes that formed so important a part of their food, to making the family bread, compounding the far-famed York-shire tea-cake and oaten scones, cutting up meat for hash, and cooking broths for sick cottagers,—her tuition was strict and exact. She made dainty housewives of them all by the time Maria was ten and Charlotte seven.

A graphic picture of the group of father and children at this date occurs in a letter from Mr. Brontë to Charlotte's friend and biographer, Mrs. Gaskell. It has been often quoted, but my story would be incomplete without it, not only because it exhibits, as no other narrator has been able to show, the radical peculiarities of the father's sys-tem of education, and the characteristics of each child, already marked, but because it places the teacher in a more amiable light than that in which we are generally dis-posed to regard him.

" When mere children, as soon as they could read and write, Charlotte and her brother and sisters used to invent and act little plays of their own, in which the Duke of Wellington, my daughter Charlotte's hero, was sure to come off conqueror ; when a dispute would not infrequently arise amongst them regarding the compara-tive merits of him, Buonaparte, Hannibal, and Cæsar. When the argument got warm, and rose to its height, as their mother was dead, I had sometimes to come in as arbitrator, and settle the dispute according to the best of my judgment.   .   .   .

"When—as far as I can remember—the oldest was about ten years of age and the youngest about four, thinking that they knew more than I had yet discovered, in order to make them speak with less timidity, I deemed that if they were put under a sort of cover I might gain my end, and, happening to have a mask in the house, I told them all to stand and speak boldly from under cover of the mask.

"I began with the youngest (Anne, afterwards Acton Bell) and asked 'what a child like her most wanted.' She answered, 'Age and experience.' I asked the next (Emily, afterwards Ellis Bell) what I had best do with her brother Branwell, who was sometimes a naughty boy. She answered, 'Reason with him, and when he won't listen to reason, whip him!' I asked Branwell 'what was the best way of knowing the difference between the intellects of man and woman.' He answered, 'By considering the difference between them as to their bodies.' I then asked Charlotte 'what was the best book in the world.' She answered, 'The Bible.' 'And what was the next best?' She answered, 'The Book of Nature.' I then asked next 'what was the best mode of education for a woman.' She answered, 'That which would make her rule her house well.'

"Lastly, I asked the oldest (Maria) 'what was the best mode of spending time.' She answered, 'By laying it out in preparation for a happy Eternity.'

"I may not have given precisely their words, but I have nearly done so, as they made a deep and lasting impression on my memory. The substance, however, was exactly what I have stated."

## CHAPTER IV

### SCHOOL LIFE AT COWAN BRIDGE

THE winter of 1823–24 brought increase of care to Miss Branwell, and anxiety to her brother-in-law. Measles and whooping-cough were prevalent in Haworth, and the children at the Parsonage did not escape infection. Maria and Elizabeth had both diseases at once, and coughed far into the spring. The younger children rallied more quickly. The convalescence of the older sisters may have been retarded by their sedentary habits and closer confinement to the house. The bracing air of the upper moors would be recommended as a specific for whooping-cough by the modern country practitioner.

While the four lesser children raced over the heather and spent all their half-holidays under the open sky, Maria and Elizabeth sat and sewed with their aunt upon the outfit they were to take with them to school the first of July.

The home-circle was to be broken at last ; the moorland nest was stirred. Father, aunt, Mr. Brontë's clerical brethren, and their benevolent consorts, were agreed as to the expediency of sending the girls to boarding-school. They were bright learners, undoubtedly, and in one way and another had acquired, if they had not assimilated, an enormous amount of miscellaneous information, most of which would be utterly useless in future life. They had no accomplishments, and proficiency in these was not attainable in Haworth. Their father could teach them Greek and Latin, but not French or German, music and drawing. If they would not be at a hopeless disadvantage when compared with other girls and young women of their station, a change was imperatively needed.

The school indicated by Providence, and an advisory committee of the aforementioned well-wishers, had been in successful operation for a year at the village of Cowan Bridge, not far from Leeds. It was founded by a clergyman, and was what we would

stigmatise as "a half-charitable organisation," designed expressly for the daughters
of impecunious clergymen. Mr. Brontë
had five girls and a small income. For
fifteen pounds a year each of his daughters
could be taught grammar, writing, arith-
metic, all kinds of needlework, with a
practical knowledge of clear starching
and laundrywork in general, history, geography, with the use of the globes, and for
three pounds more, music or drawing. The
uniform of the school was adapted to the
slender means of the semi-patrons, semi-
beneficiaries, whose offspring were to reap
the advantages of the institution: white
frocks on Sunday, nankeen on week-days;
purple stuff frocks, with cloth cloaks of
the same colour, in winter. The outfit
of frock, cloak, bonnet, tippet, and frills
was furnished by the trustees, each pupil
bringing three pounds for the purchase
thereof.

Moderate as the terms sound, it was
necessary for Mr. Brontë to pay one hundred and eighty dollars yearly for his two
girls, thirty dollars more if they wished to
study music or drawing. The Haworth
living has never, I am told, been worth

more than two hundred and fifty pounds per annum, and while money went farther then than now, a family of eight people, and two, or even one servant, must have practised strict economy to avoid running into debt.

An old woman, a former parishioner of Mr. Brontë, described some of these frugal methods to me. She said that all the household sewing was done by Miss Branwell and her nieces, even to making their own dresses. The girls, after they were grown, wore the same bonnets, without alteration of shape or trimming, for two years. The gowns and other clothing of the children were invariably whole and clean, but each article was mended as long as it would hold together ; their linen undergarments were darned by a thread until the original fabric scarcely appeared at all. They knit their own stockings and when holes were worn in them, imitated the stitch in darning after the Belgian fashion of which Caroline Helstone complained in *Shirley*.

How many heart-tremblings and qualms of prospective homesickness and yearnings over the dear ones to be left behind went with the stitching of chemises and gathering of petticoats and hemming of handkerchiefs, while the "little mother" and her almost twin in age wrought under their aunt's eye through the lengthening afternoons formerly devoted to roaming and dreaming aloud to one another, out of hearing of unsympathetic listeners, — it pains us to the heart to imagine. It is easy, as a rule, to transplant young shoots. These had struck their roots so deep that removal was agony.

In my humble, individual opinion, the best boarding-school is a poor substitute for a tolerably good home. The "half-charity" at Cowan Bridge was a new organisation, unseasoned, and stiff in the hinges. After weighing the *pros* and *cons* of the controversy that raged over the subject after the publication of *Jane Eyre* and Mrs. Gaskell's *Life of Charlotte Brontë*, the impartial judge must credit much that Charlotte wrote of "Lowood" and her biographer's corroboration of the same. There was all too much truth in the stories of badly cooked food, unkind (probably because cheap) under-teachers, and such evils of drainage and dampness as led to the low fever that broke out in the school in 1825.

I have said that in Helen Burns Charlotte embodied tender and mournful recollections of the "little mother" who had guided her first tottering footsteps, and left the image of a saintly martyr in her heart and soul. Whether the fare at Cowan Bridge school were good, as the defenders of the institution assert, or bad, as Charlotte told Mrs. Gaskell it was, and made the worse "by the dirty carelessness of the cook, so that she and her sisters disliked their meals exceedingly,"—there is no doubt that Maria's sojourn there was a period of suffering, borne with angelic patience. She was "delicate, unusually clever and thoughtful for her age, gentle, and—untidy." Her mother had had no time to train her in habits of orderly neatness, with five other children racing upon the heels of the first-born, and since the child was able to run alone she had been too busy looking after the younger babies to think of herself. She had a cough when she entered the school, and it never left her. Charlotte tells us—and she never exaggerated the truth—that the sisters, used to the dainty simplicity of the Parsonage table, were hungry all the time they were at Cowan Bridge. The porridge was often scorched; the rice- and custard-puddings were made with rain-water from a cistern that caught the wash from the roofs; so-called meat-pies were composed of the scrapings of plates and dishes, and the milk tasted of the unwashed pans in which it was kept. Maria studied far beyond her strength and was frequently ill, especially as the winter approached, and the racking cough everybody took as a natural sequel of last winter's illness, wore upon lungs and nerves.

An under-teacher, branded with infamy by Charlotte as " Miss Scatcherd," slept in a small chamber opening out of the fireless dormitory, and one morning when Maria, whose side had been blistered a day or so before to avert pleurisy, was slowly putting on her stockings in bed, "Miss Scatcherd issued from her room, and without asking for a word of explanation from the sick and frightened girl, took her by the arm, on the side to which the blister had been applied, and whirled her out into the middle of the floor, abusing her all the time, for dirty and untidy habits." Mrs. Gaskell had the tale from an eye-witness, and it agrees well with Charlotte's description of what her sister endured.

Elizabeth, of whom we hear less than of the others, fared better when she was laid up for some days by a severe cut upon the head. The superintendent—" Miss Temple" of *Jane Eyre*—kept her in her own room and took care of her until she was able to be about. From this lady we learn that the second daughter bore her suffering with the "exemplary patience" that was a family trait, and won much upon her nurse's esteem. The passing allusion to Elizabeth and her restful seclusion in the teacher's room is the one gleam of light in the Cowan Bridge episode, and it is faint enough.

The two elder sisters seem to have made no complaint at home of food or teachers, or it was not considered worthy of attention if such were entered, for Charlotte and Emily were enrolled as pupils in September. The latter is said by Miss Temple to have been "a darling child, under five years of age, and quite the pet nursling of the school." Charlotte is referred to as "a bright, clever little child."

So bright, as the event proved, that nothing escaped her eyes, and nothing was lost from the retentive memory. So clever that her picture of these, the first months she had spent out of her home, is as sharp and vivid as an artist's proof etching from a master's hand.

"We had to pass an hour every day in the open air. Our clothing was insufficient to protect us from the severe cold. We had no boots ; the snow got into our shoes and melted there ; our ungloved hands became numbed and covered with chilblains, as were our feet. I remember well the distracting irritation I endured from this cause every evening, when my feet inflamed, and the torture of thrusting the swelled, raw, and stiff toes into my shoes in the morning. Then, the scanty supply of food was distressing. With the keen appetites of growing children, we had scarcely sufficient to keep alive a delicate invalid. Whenever the famished great girls had an opportunity, they would coax or menace the little ones out of their portion. Many a time I have shared between two claimants the precious morsel of brown bread distributed at tea-time, and, after relinquishing to a third half the contents of my mug of coffee, I have swallowed the remainder with an accompaniment of secret tears, forced from me by the exigency of hunger.

"Sundays were dreary days in that wintry season. We had to walk two miles to church. We set out cold ; we arrived at church colder. During the morning service we became almost paralysed. It was too far to return to dinner, and an allowance of cold meat and

4

bread, in the same penurious proportion observed in our
daily meals, was served round between the services.

" At the close of the afternoon service we returned by
an exposed and hilly road, where the bitter winter wind,
blowing over a range of snowy summits to the north,
almost flayed the skin from our faces.

" How we longed for the light and heat of a blazing
fire when we got back !  But to the little ones, at
least, this was denied.  Each hearth in the schoolroom
was immediately surrounded by a double row of great
girls, and behind them the younger children crouched
in groups, wrapping their starved arms in their pinafores.

" A little solace came at tea-time in the shape of a
double ration of bread—a whole, instead of a half-slice—
with the delicious addition of a thin scrape of butter.
It was the hebdomadal treat to which we all looked
forward from Sabbath to Sabbath.  I generally contrived
to reserve a moiety of this bounteous repast for myself,
but the remainder I was invariably obliged to part with."

Should it seem incredible that Mr Brontë
and Miss Branwell, but half-a-day's journey
distant from Cowan Bridge, suspected nothing of privations which endangered the
girls' lives, we must hark back to other accounts of the singular unconcern manifested
at that day by parents in every rank of
society with respect to the school experiences of their children.  They were passed
over, body and soul, to instructors paid to
conduct their education.  Punishments were

severe, and, to our notion, barbarous in variety and ingenuity. The ferule, the rod, dunce-cap and stool, the dark room, fasting upon bread and water for a week at a time, —were some of the commonest and mildest penances inflicted for imperfect lessons, untidiness, and trivial lapses in speech and deportment. Home letters were supervised before they were posted, and any symptom of discontent was summarily punished. All of this belonged to the educational system which found favour in our forefathers' eyes, and is affectionately alluded to by purblind sentimentalists of our generation as " the good old times."

Furthermore, let us consider the improbability that the four Haworth exiles formulated any complaint against school and teachers. Charlotte explains their submission to the grievous present in one sentence uttered by Helen Burns.

" You must wish to leave Lowood ? " queries Jane Eyre.

" No. Why should I ? I was sent to Lowood to get an education, and it would be of no use going away until I have attained that object."

The love of learning for learning's sake

was already a passion with the home-bred pupils, so much older in mind than in body. In words that to our imaginations burn and throb along the printed page, Charlotte depicts the unfolding of her intellect and fancy under the tuition she received that otherwise dour and fateful winter.   As we read, we are reminded of the efflorescence of some gorgeous tropical plant, in its native soil, and in the fulness of its own season.   Biting cold, pinching hunger, and small tyrannies are forgotten or minimised.

"I toiled hard, and my success was proportionate to my efforts.   My memory, not naturally tenacious, improved with practice ; exercise sharpened my wits.   In a few weeks I was promoted to a .higher class ; in less than two months I was allowed to commence French and drawing.   I learned the first two tenses of the verb *Être* and sketched my first cottage on the same day. That night, on going to bed, I forgot to prepare in imagination the Barmecide supper of hot roast potatoes, or white bread and new milk, with which I was wont to amuse my inward cravings.   I feasted, instead, on the spectacle of ideal drawings which I saw in the dark ; all the work of my own hands ; freely pencilled houses and trees, picturesque rocks and ruins, Cuyp-like groups of cattle, sweet paintings of butterflies hovering over unblown roses, of birds picking at ripe cherries, of wrens' nests enclosing pearl-like eggs, wreathed about with young ivy sprays.   I examined, too, in thought, the possibility of my ever being able to translate currently a certain little French story-book which Madame Pierrot had, that day, shown me ;—nor was that problem solved to my satisfaction ere I fell sweetly asleep."

# CHAPTER V

## DEATHS OF MARIA AND ELIZABETH—MARIA'S SUCCESSOR—FIRESIDE CONCLAVES

"I have not the least hesitation in saying that, upon the whole, the comforts were as many and the privations as few at Cowan Bridge as can well be found in so large an establishment. How far young, or delicate, children are able to contend with the necessary evils of a public school is, in my opinion, a very grave question, and does not enter into the present discussion."

The extract from the letter of a former teacher in the Cowan Bridge School, while offered in vindication of the founder and managers of the institution in question, leaves the case of the Brontë sisters to the judgment of those who have heard Charlotte's version of it, and Mrs. Gaskell's sifting of the evidence laid before her at a much later date.

The four daughters of the Haworth clergyman were altogether too young and too delicate to be subjected to the obvious chances and rude changes of a boarding-school conducted upon strictly economical principles, even had their previous training been that of the ordinary little girl of the period, born and bred in a rural parsonage.

A low fever, approximating typhus, appeared among the pupils in the spring of 1825. Charlotte's account of the dread visitant is doubtless as accurate as it is thrilling. The opening sentence frames the picture :

" That forest-dell, where Lowood lay, was the cradle of fog and fog-bred pestilence, which, quickening with the quickening spring, crept into the Orphan Asylum, breathed typhus through its crowded schoolroom and dormitory, and, ere May arrived, transformed the seminary into a hospital."

In the stricter surveillance of the girls' health consequent upon the alarm, Maria Brontë's condition came under the notice of attendant physicians. She had escaped the fever, but was pronounced to be far gone in consumption. Her father, summoned imperatively, was amazed and horrified at finding her changed almost beyond recognition since he had last seen her, and hurried her home without a day's delay. She was lifted into the Leeds coach, propped against pillows, and her sisters kissed for the last time the white face pitifully wasted and small, lighted by great eyes whose " singular beauty was of meaning, of movement, of radiance." The eyes rested that night upon the home for which she had longed in unuttered and unutterable heart-sickness through the year of exile. The breath of the moors, the pure sweep of the wind over the dear and remembered hills, could not fill the shattered lungs. For less than a week she lay, smiling and patient, in the chamber where her mother had languished for so long, awaiting the summons for which the name-daughter now listened ; looking through the same window upon the square tower silhouetted against the sky. Maria passed quietly away on the sixth of May, and was buried beside her mother under the church floor.

Less than a fortnight afterward, the coach stopped at Cowan Bridge Seminary for another sick child. The authorities, awakened from apathy by the tidings of Maria Brontë's death so soon after leaving the school as to disparage the sanitary conditions of the place, or the care she had had there, were uneasy at Elizabeth's racking cough and the clear pallor of her complexion. Medical examination showed that she, also, was in the last stages of phthisis. She was made ready hurriedly and sent off to Haworth under the care of a trustworthy attendant. News of her death on June 15th reached Charlotte and Emily just before the midsummer holidays to which they were looking forward with feverish eagerness.

It passes our understanding, knowing what we do, at this distance from the time and scene of the piteous little tragedy, that Mr. Brontë should have returned the two girls to Cowan Bridge in September. Partial elucidation is furnished by the teacher's letter from which an extract was made awhile ago.

"During both these visits" (*i. e.*, when he brought Maria and Elizabeth in July, and again Charlotte and Emily in September, 1824) "Mr. Brontë lodged at the school, sat at the same table with the children, saw the whole routine of the establishment, and, so far as I have ever known, was satisfied with everything that came under his observation."

" *The two younger children enjoyed uni-
formly good health,*" is an italicised sentence that weakens the force of that which
preceded it when we learn that both
these younger children were taken from the
school before the winter closed in. " It
was evident that the damp situation of the
house at Cowan Bridge did not suit their
health." We hope it was the father who
took alarm at the unchildlike gravity that,
like a frost in springtime, had struck the
brightness out of Charlotte's face, and at
the spiritless diligence with which she performed tasks in which she formerly revelled.

She cherished the memory of her dead
sisters as long as she lived as "wonders of
talent and kindness." She gave Maria im-
mortality as "Helen Burns." Called suddenly and terribly to take the eldest sister's
place to the three whom Maria had borne
in her arms and her heart from the hour of
their birth until the day when Branwell and
Anne were lifted to her bed for a farewell
kiss from her stiffening lips—Charlotte left
childhood behind her forever. Mrs. Gaskell says "the duties that now fell upon
her seemed almost like a legacy from the
gentle little sufferer."

What Maria had suffered in the ungenial atmosphere of the semi-charity school was burned into Charlotte's mind, as witness *Jane Eyre*. Maria's motherly solicitude, her graces of mind and heart, the singular absence of low and selfish motives in all that she said and did, made up an exemplar which her successor in the home strove, in the like unselfish spirit, to follow.

The home-coming in the late autumn, when the hillsides were "livid," when the plover had gone southward, and the hardier swifts flew low in the gusty afternoons, was comfort rather than happiness. In the long walks, at once resumed and never discontinued by her as girl and woman, it was Charlotte who looked after the feebler children, repressed Branwell's sauciness, and mediated between him and Emily,—his "chum" among his sisters, yet the one with whom he oftenest quarrelled. The lessons in the father's study were taken up as if they had never been laid aside,—Branwell and Anne bringing the class back to the original size. Miss Branwell drilled her nieces in thrift and needlework. A middle-aged Haworth woman, wiry in body as in character, was installed as maid-of-all-work, and as "our Tabby," in time, got all of the household, the master not excepted, under her kindly yet despotic rule.

Now and then, a clergyman from the neighbourhood, or from a distant parish, took dinner or tea with Mr. Brontë, or some school-meeting or clerical conference in the Haworth Church brought a batch of five or six to dine, sup, and sleep at the Parsonage. At such times "the children" sat at table, and about the fire in the evenings, hearkening with open ears and non-committal faces to the professional talk, —each, all unsuspected by the subjects of the mental criticism, taking notes for future use. Other glimpses of what lay beyond the girdling hills they loved, they had none, save through books and newspapers.

"We take two, and see three, newspapers a week," wrote Charlotte in her diary, complacently. "We take the *Leeds Intelligencer,* a most excellent Tory newspaper, and the *Leeds Mercury,* Whig, edited by Mr. Baines, and his brother, son-in-law, and his two sons, Edward and Talbot. We see the *John Bull ;* it is a high Tory, very violent. Mr. Driver lends us it, as likewise *Blackwoods' Magazine,* the most able periodical there is. The editor is Mr. Christopher North, an old man, seventy-four years of age ; the 1st of April is his birth-day. His company are Timothy Tickler, Morgan

O'Doherty, Macrabin Mordecai, Mullion, Warnell, and
James Hogg, a man of most extraordinary genius, a
Scottish shepherd."

The bookish talk is only redeemed from
priggishness by the grave simplicity of the
juvenile critic. Books and periodicals were
more alive to her than the inhabitants of
the next parish. The story goes in the
village that all four of the Parsonage children were once invited to a child's birthday
party at the house of one of the small gentry in the neighbourhood. Then and there
they underwent agonies of discomfort, first
from bashfulness, and then from finding
themselves the focus of twenty pairs of
eyes, some pitying, some contemptuous,
all amazed at the discovery that the three
girls and one boy knew not one children's
game—not even " Hunt the Slipper," or
" Round about the Gooseberry Bush."

We can imagine the indignant warmth
of the discussion upon the events of the
afternoon that went on over the kitchen
fire that night, with perhaps Tabby as a
sympathetic listener. She counted for
nothing in the conclaves never held in the
hearing of father or aunt. We may be
sure that " Slipper" and " Gooseberry

Bush " fared ill by comparison with their home diversions.

"Our plays were established ;—*Young Men*, June, 1826 " (just a year after Elizabeth's death), wrote the bookish diarist ; " *Our Fellows*, July, 1827 ; *Islanders*, December, 1827. These are our three great plays that are not kept secret. Emily's and my best plays were established the first of December, 1827 ; the others', March, 1828. Best plays mean secret plays ; they are very nice ones. All our plays are very strange ones."

Like the brains that invented, and the wits that carried them on. We are still in the dark as to the *modus operandi* of each after reading further :

" I will try to sketch out the origin of our plays more explicitly if I can. First : *Young Men*.—Papa bought Branwell some wooden soldiers at Leeds. When Papa came home it was night, and we were in bed, so next morning Branwell came to our door with a box of soldiers. Emily and I jumped out of bed, and I snatched up one, and exclaimed—' This is the Duke of Wellington ! This shall be the Duke ! ' When I had said this, Emily likewise took up one and said it should be hers ; when Anne came down, she said one should be hers. Mine was the prettiest of the whole, and the tallest, and the most perfect in every part. Emily's was a grave-looking fellow, and we called him ' Gravey.' Anne's was a queer little thing, much like herself, and we called him ' Waiting Boy.' Branwell chose his, and called him ' Buonaparte.' "

The date of this entry in Charlotte's journal is 1829, when she was thirteen years old.

As naturally as the oak is evolved from the acorn, living in books as with human companions led to the writing of books. The children had always been silent and repressed indoors. When pent up in the hall-room upstairs by days of continuous storm, they were as quiet now as when Maria hushed their prattle to whispers and enjoined them to laugh low because "poor mamma" was ill in the adjoining room. The aunt, "clicking about the stone stairs and halls in pattens," must have smiled contentedly in passing the closed door of what was never "the nursery" after Anne's cradle was taken away. After all, the children did credit to her training. If she glanced in at them occasionally, from the force of habit and conscience, she saw nothing unusual in their occupations. Paper, pencil, book, and pen were to them what doll-houses, kites, tops, and whips were to other girls and boys. Charlotte covered hundreds of pages of copy-books and the blank ends of old letters with minute characters one requires the aid of a magnifying-glass to decipher. Her favourite study was the broad, high window-seat. Curled up like a kitten, she would write for hours without speaking, holding her paper close to her near-sighted eyes, a trick she was not cured of at Cowan Bridge. Emily sat on the floor, using her knees for a desk. Branwell would sprawl at full length, his chin supported by his hand, the book from which he read, or the paper on which he wrote, on the floor before him. Even little Anne scribbled stories with a pencil in "coarse hand"—as writing-teachers called it a generation back—by the time she was five years old.

The scene is eerie as we sketch it to ourselves,—the uncanny group of small immortals, whose childhood was surely unlike any other ever lived in Christian and modern times; the intent faces and dreamful eyes bent over busy fingers; the brooding silence, unbroken save by the moan of the wind and the plashing rain against the panes. What Charlotte saw when she raised her head to gaze through the window, she painted a score of years later, in a few masterly strokes:

"There is only one cloud in the sky ; but it curtains it from pole to pole. The wind cannot rest ; it hurries

sobbing over hills of sullen outline, colourless with
twilight and mist.    Rain has beat all day on that
church-tower.    It rises dark from the stony enclosure of
its church-yard ; the nettles, the long grass, and the
tombs, all drip with wet."

The little parallelogram of dooryard between the Parsonage and the then treeless
burial-ground, paved with weather-black-
ened tombstones, is now filled with shrub-
bery and flowers.  When Charlotte surveyed
it in the musing intervals of composition,
a clump of stunted currant-bushes, some
dwarf evergreens, and, on the wall, a patch
of ivy, were all that relieved the monotone
of grey and black.  Right before her was
the door in the wall which had been un-
locked but three times since they came to
Haworth to live, and would not be opened
again until another coffin was ready to be
borne through, down the sloping path to
the church porch.  Such was the custom
of the region.  The mute *memento mori*
faced the door by which the living went in
and out of their temporary dwelling in
business pertaining to the life that now is.

5

# CHAPTER VI

## MISS WOOLER'S SCHOOL—MARY TAYLOR
## AND ELLEN NUSSEY

AMONG the incidents transmitted to us tending to prove that Mr. Brontë was not so indifferent to his children's happiness or so unobservant of their occupations as we have inclined to believe, we note two belonging to the five years spent by Charlotte under his tutelage after her return from Cowan Bridge in the autumn of 1825.

One has been given in her account of the origin of the "strange plays" invented by the four. If the father had a favourite in the flock it was his only son,—the handsomest, and reckoned by family and neighbours to be the most brilliant of them all. The girls had no dolls, but a box of toy-soldiers was brought from Leeds for the petted boy. Still the father offered no ob-

HAWORTH CHURCH BEFORE RESTORATION

jection to the division of the puppets for the furtherance of the "play" of *Young Men.*

Mr. Shorter tells of a sixpenny blank-book given to Charlotte by her father, on the cover of which is written :

"*All that is written in this book must be in a good, plain, and legible hand.—P. B.*"

He was cognisant, then, of the scribbling propensities of his daughter, had probably had a glimpse of the MSS. done in microscopic characters, and gave a broad hint as to his wishes on that head.

The earliest date affixed to any of the Brontë manuscripts is upon—as we observe with surprise—an "exceedingly childish production," or so says Mr. Shorter, "*By P. B. Brontë.*" The title is *The Battle of Washington,* and there are "full-page coloured illustrations." It was written in 1827, Branwell being then ten years old. From babyhood he fancied himself, and was believed by his kindred, to be an artist born.

Charlotte made no such claim for herself, but her passionate love of the beautiful, the artistic tastes she had no opportunity to indulge, and, above all, the strong necessity

of expression that consumed her like a restless fire, impelled her to use pencil with
pen.   Every engraving or sketch that came
in her way was examined critically by the
short-sighted eyes until she had seen all
that was in it, and much that would escape
an ordinary spectator.   At this time she
had a hope, secret and strenuous, of becoming an artist, and practised drawing
with painstaking assiduity.   Knowing nothing of rules and methods except from the
few lessons she had had at Cowan Bridge,
she set herself to copying engravings, line
for line, work for which the long, delicate
fingers of her tiny hands were especially
adapted.

"Stippling, I believe they call it," she
wrote afterward of the misdirected labour.
"I thought it very fine at the time."

> "Oh, I feel like a seed in the cold earth,
>   Quickening at heart, and pining for the air!"

The lines recur to us continually in following the course of her life, so tame upon the
surface, so tumultuous within.

A quarter-mile or more down the street
closed by churchyard and Parsonage, lived
a joiner and cabinet-maker—a character in

his way, and with a warm side to his
heart for the "Parson's children." His
shop, on the second floor of his house, saw
them more frequently than the interior of
any other dwelling in the village. Hardly
a week passed in which one or the other,
sometimes all four, of the shy, grave-eyed
students did not appear in the upper room
—redolent of newly cut woods, paint, and
varnish. They were always bound upon
one errand. A picture in pencil or water-
colours needed a frame, and a bargain was
to be struck with Mr. Wood for it. With
true Yorkshire and Brontë-esque independence, not one of the artists would accept
the frame as a gift. A piece of his or her
own work was to be bartered for what was
needed. As the frames were to be made
of odd corners left over from larger pictures,
scraps of cornices, door and window cas-
ings, at second hand, or which had been
cast aside as unavailable for other purposes
by the workman, he would gladly have
donated the materials and glued them into
the requisite form for the pleasure of serv-
ing the "odd, clever creatures." He knew
them too well, and had too much native
tact, to insist upon this point. So with

genuine breeding and kindness, he accepted the poor little daub or scrawl, hunted up suitable stuff for the frame that was to enclose the picture reserved by the owner, and accounted it a business transaction.

"He had a drawerful of the pictures he got in this way," his daughter told me. "When the young gentleman got older and could really paint, he did several large pictures for my father in exchange for bigger frames. One of these frames—quite large and heavy—was intended for a picture painted for Mr. Brontë. The subject was *Jacob's Ladder*. Mr. Brontë thought so much of it that he hung it over his study mantel. One night, a candle was left accidentally too near it, and a corner of the frame took fire. You can see the painting in the Brontë Museum."

From this family I heard a warm vindication of Mr. Brontë from the charge of excessive harshness to his motherless children, and neglect of their wants and feelings. Here, too, I had the same testimony I had gathered from other parishioners, to his popularity with the poorer classes, and his indulgence in monetary matters. Whatever the people wanted they got if he could grant it. When the tithes were not paid, he would not press pew-renters for them. Sometimes he lost as much as £100 per

annum by his "easy ways." That was
one reason he was always poor.

The agèd widow of Mr. Wood repeated
the story others had given me of Branwell's many and dazzling gifts of mind and
person. She had seen him, again and
again, write two letters at once, one with
each hand, talking brightly all the time
upon a third subject—"Poor lad! He
might have been anything he pleased, if
he had only kept steady! I have wished,
often and often, that we had kept the
children's bits of drawings. They would
be interesting now."

I cared not a jot for *Jacob's Ladder*, having seen enough of Branwell's pictures—all
more or less wretched—to slake any curi-
osity I may have felt on that head. I should
have liked to have a peep at Charlotte's
"stipplings" and the free-hand sketches
by means of which she strove to make
thought visible.

She catalogues twenty-two books written by herself in those five years of housework, desultory study, and browsing in her
father's library of English classics ; of por-
ing over political leaders, news of the nations, and literary reviews in the few

newspapers which they saw, and " *Black-wood's Magazine*, the most able periodical there is." Some of her writings are in two volumes, some in three, some in four. There are tales, autobiographies, travels, political disquisitions, ballads and short poems, a drama, an epic, conversations,— all engrossed in the clear, small script that tantalises the average eyesight ; thousands upon thousands of words, written because she must write, and with no ulterior thought of publication.

The *Young Men's Magazine*, in six numbers, was *printed* with a pen by Charlotte for circulation in the "study," her two sisters and her brother constituting the whole number of subscribers and readers. Not one word of the tens of thousands was read to father or aunt. So long as the children were quiet and not in mischief, Miss Branwell did not trouble herself with their doings out of work-hours, and Mr. Brontë was more self-absorbed with each passing year of widowerhood.

When Charlotte was fifteen he awoke to the conviction that she was no longer one of the children, and bestirred himself to find a school where she could be fitted to do a woman's part in the working-day world. His choice fell, happily for all concerned, upon Miss Margaret Wooler's boarding-home for girls at Roe Head, a commodious country-house standing in its own grounds a little back from the Leeds coach-road, about twenty miles from Haworth.

The physical features of the two neighbourhoods are as unlike as if they were twenty leagues apart. The visitor to the sun-warmed slopes and pleasant pastures of the contiguous manor of Kirklees, in the heart of whose "immemorial wood" Robin Hood is said to be buried, turns, for the most graphic picture of the scene, to Charlotte's sketch of it in *Shirley*:

" They looked down on the deep valley robed in May raiment ; on varied meads, some pearled with daisies, and some golden with king-cups. To-day all this young verdure smiled clear in sunlight ; transparent emerald and amber gleams played over it. On Nunnwood " (Kirklees) "—the sole remnant of antique British forest in a region whose lowlands were once all sylvan chase, as its highlands were breast-deep heather—slept the shadow of a cloud ; the distant hills were dappled ; the horizon was shaded and tinted like mother-of-pearl ; silvery blues, soft purples, evanescent greens and rose-shades, all melting into fleeces of white cloud, pure as azure snow—allured the eye as with a remote glimpse of heaven's foundations. The air blowing on the green brow of the Common was fresh, and sweet, and bracing."

Beauty of this type was as new to the Haworth recluse as the friendships she was to form at Roe Head with Miss Wooler and the two girls who came to know her better than any other human beings ever did, except her sisters. Mary Taylor and Ellen Nussey were already domesticated in Miss Wooler's household when Charlotte was entered as a pupil. The Taylor sisters, Mary and Martha, were the daughters of a Yorkshire banker whose country-seat was but three miles from Roe Head. Charlotte has drawn the family with strength and spirit in *Shirley* as the "Yorkes." The fidelity of the portraiture is vouched for by one of Mary's brothers, the "Martin" of the novel, to whom the chapter depicting the household was submitted in MS. His only adverse criticism was that she "had not drawn them strongly enough."

Mary, the elder of the girls, was "Rose Yorke"; Martha was "Jessie." Miss Wooler thought Mary "too pretty to live" when she was brought to her school. Charlotte describes Mary's face as

" not harsh, nor yet quite pretty. It is simple—childlike in feature; the round cheeks bloom ; as to the grey eyes, they are otherwise than childlike—a serious soul lights them. . . . She has a mind full-set, thick-sown with the germs of ideas her mother never knew. It is agony to her often to have these ideas trampled on and repressed. She has never rebelled yet ; but, if hard-driven, she will rebel one day, and then it will be once for all."

As a pendant to this crayon-sketch, we have Mary's picture of Charlotte, as she saw her on a raw mid-January morning in the year 1831:

" I first saw her coming out of a covered cart, in very old-fashioned clothes, and looking very cold and miser-able. She was coming to school at Miss Wooler's. When she appeared in the school-room, her dress was changed, but just as old. She looked a little old woman, so short-sighted that she always appeared to be seeking something, and moving her head from side to side to catch a sight of it. She was very shy and nervous, and spoke with a strong Irish accent. When a book was given her, she dropped her head over it till her nose nearly touched it, and when she was told to hold her head up, up went the book after it, still close to her nose, so that it was not possible to help laughing." *

On the same day Charlotte Brontë and Ellen Nussey (the " Caroline Helstone " of

* Mrs. Gaskell's *Life of Charlotte Brontë.*

*Shirley*) met for the first time. This young girl, then near Charlotte's own age—fifteen, lived with her brothers at Brookroyd, a fine old homestead four miles from Roe Head. Biographers are agreed that Charlotte drew no more correct portrait—and she never failed of "catching a likeness"—than in "Caroline Helstone," albeit the lonely, dependent niece of the austere rector of Briarfield differed widely in environment from the petted member of a large family, and with whom life had gone upon velvet from her babyhood. I give the portrait as Charlotte has painted it, love prompting each touch. As we read we can see a tender smile lighting up the great red-hazel eyes, of which Mrs. Gaskell says, "I never saw the like in any other human creature."

"It was not absolutely necessary to know her in order to like her. She was fair enough to please, even at the first view. Her shape suited her age; it was girlish, light, and pliant; every curve was neat, every limb proportionate; her face was expressive and gentle; her eyes were handsome, and gifted, at times, with a winning beam that stole into the heart, with a language that spoke softly to the affections. Her mouth was very pretty; she had a delicate skin, and a fine flow of brown hair which she knew how to arrange with taste; curls became her, and she possessed them in picturesque profusion. Her style of dress announced taste in the wearer ; very unobtrusive in fashion, far from costly in material, but suitable in colour to the fair complexion with which it contrasted, and in make to the slight form which it draped."

Coming softly, as it was her wont to move, into the schoolroom at the noon recess, Ellen espied a small figure shrinking into the recess of a window overlooking the playground. The ten or dozen girls who then composed the family-school were pelting one another with snowballs in the courtyard, their shrieks of laughter ringing clearly through the frozen air. The new pupil was crying quietly, wiping the tears furtively as they dropped, although she thought herself unseen. Her dress was uncouth, herself miserably bashful, as lost and forlorn as if the carrier's covered cart that had left her "to be called for," at Roe Head, had dumped her upon another planet.

Did the memory of the interview that followed steal over the mind of the successful author when she wrote :—"Caroline had tact, and she had fine instinct. She felt that Rose Yorke was a peculiar child—one of the unique. She knew how to treat her."

So well did Ellen Nussey know how to treat the desolate waif blown thither from the moorland Parsonage, that she found her way right speedily to the sealed fountain of the stranger's heart, and kept her place there until it was chilled by death.

As was to be expected, the Haworth girl's ignorance of text-books and conventional "education" was a woful stumbling-block for a time to her advancement. Had Miss Wooler been the ordinary type of teacher, the drawback might have been almost fatal to the ambition to excel in her studies that inspired Charlotte to conquer homesickness and aversion to new associations. She spoke with prim correctness, she wrote clear, nervous English, but she knew not one rule of English grammar. She had devoured all the books of travel she could get hold of, and several of her own composition were in the *Catalogue of My Books, with the Date of their Completion,* yet every child in the second class at Miss Wooler's had "gone further" in geography than she. That she was not classed with the "little girls" was due to her overwhelming distress when Miss Wooler delicately hinted her fear that it would have to be done, and to that sensible and tender-hearted woman's decision to give the odd duckling a fair chance to show what was in her. She was ranged, then, with Mary Taylor and Ellen Nussey, and the trio soon found and kept their places in the advance-guard of the home-school. Charlotte became the story-teller of the little band, as she had been to her larger audience at Cowan Bridge, beguiling wet out-of-school hours of tedium by telling tales from the *Young Men's Magazine* and " out of her own head," and keeping her roommates awake into the forbidden hours by blood-curdling romances and ghost-stories. While the rest frolicked in the courtyard she sat under a tree, dividing her attention between a book, and the clouds in the sky, the lights and shadows of the landscape. When urged to take a hand in a ball-game, she acquiesced with amiable indifference, but soon dropped out because she could not see the ball when tossed high. In muscle she was flaccid, in motion languid unless excited to self-forgetfulness. She ate little of anything, and no meat at all.

Once, Mary Taylor, redundant in vitality,

and impatient of physical feebleness, told
her new friend, with the frank brutality of
the British schoolgirl, that she was homely
and awkward.   Long afterward she reminded Charlotte of the rudeness and
begged her forgiveness.

"You did me good, Polly, so don't re-
pent of it!" was the reply, fraught with
meaning which Mary could appreciate,
knowing her as she did.

Then, as always, Charlotte was absolutely free from personal vanity.   Everyone
who has heard of her name and fame knows
of the argument with her sisters upon the
"moral wrong" of making every heroine
beautiful, and her boast, "I will show you
a heroine as plain and as small as myself,
who shall be as interesting as any of yours."

The jesting promise was the germ of
*Jane Eyre.*

Mary Taylor was as outspoken in her surprise at the "things that were out of our
range altogether" which Charlotte knew.
She had read more books than they had
ever heard of, and forgot nothing she had
read ; was conversant with the works, and
had some knowledge of the *personnel*, of
every English author of note, speaking of

them as naturally as her comrades chatted
of their neighbours and kinspeople.

"You are always talking about clever
people — Johnson and Sheridan and the
like !" said one listener testily.

Charlotte lost the captious spirit of the
remark in the obvious incongruity of the
classification.

"You don't know the meaning of
'clever,'" she answered, in serious good
faith; and, meditatively, "Sheridan might
be clever. Yes ! Sheridan *was* clever,—
scamps often are,—but Johnson had n't a
spark of *cleverality* in him."

One cannot but wish the great Lexico-
grapher had lived to hear the coined word,
distinctive of a shade of meaning not
reached by "cleverness." The occasional
*bons mots* recalled by her intimates prove
that she would have been as brilliant in
talk as with pen, but for the stifled life she
had led with respect to everybody and
everything without the walls of the home
where alone she was ever entirely and
happily her real self.

6

# CHAPTER VII

### HOME AGAIN—BROTHER AND SISTERS

CHARLOTTE remained at Miss Wooler's school eighteen months, returning to Haworth in 1832. Limited as was the circle of pupils and teachers that represented society to her during her absence from home, it was busy, lively, and stimulating by comparison with the routine to which Emily and Anne had been bound meanwhile. Miss Branwell's "set ways" hardened into rigidity in her seclusion from the mild dissipations of Penzance tea-parties and family gatherings. In evidence of this, we are told that she never changed the style of her dress from what was "the thing" in Penzance when she left that place in 1823, and had her nieces' clothes made upon the same models. Even in Haworth they were "old-fashioned" in

their Sunday best.   Mr. Brontë had added
to this effect by bringing his daughters up
to despise fashion and finery.   So long as
their garments were whole and neat, none
of them cared how they looked in other
people's eyes.

I have heard much of this period of her
life from an old Haworth resident who
taught in the Sunday-school "turn and
turn about" with Charlotte.   That is, they
had the same class on alternate Sundays,
and of course had frequent occasion to
consult upon matters connected with the
scholars, all drawn from the working
classes.

"Neat as neat could be," is the survivor's report.
"Never a break in a shoe, or a rip in a glove.   But it
did not matter if her bonnet was four years old, and her
gowns were always made the one way.   She was very
small—hardly bigger than a child of twelve, with such
bits of hands and feet !   Pretty?   No ! I should say not
—but pleasant of face.   Her hair was light-brown—not
red, as I am told some people have said it was.   A very
pretty colour, and never out of order.   It did not curl,
and she wore it parted in the middle and brought down
each side of her face before it was put behind her ears—
as the fashion was then.   Her nose looked larger because her face was thin ; her mouth was large, too, as
you see it in her picture.   Her only good feature was
her eyes.   They were a sort of reddish-brown,—a queer

colour, but beautiful. When she talked they lighted up
until I 've seen her look almost handsome. Her voice
was pleasant, and the children liked her. She heard
them say the Catechism, and psalms, and collects, and
the like, but she never preached or talked much in the
class.

"She was not seen often in the village. Miss Branwell or Tabby did the marketing, and there was nothing
to call the Miss Brontës this way. When they walked,
it was up over the moors. They would go miles and
miles in that direction—always together, while there
were three of them ; afterward the two, and then but
the one. The walk out of the side-gate of the Parsonage and through the field at the back and so on over the
hills to the waterfall, as much as three miles away, still
goes by the name of ' Charlotte Brontë's favourite walk.'
They were not so much what I should call 'unsociable'
as reserved. You see, they were brought up by themselves, and it was n't easy to change when they were
women grown. They would speak kindly and politely
to anybody they happened to meet, and ask after sick
people, and all that. They were never stiff, or what
would be considered stuck-up. *She* was just as simple
in her ways and as friendly as ever, after she became
celebrated."


We are indebted, however, to Ellen Nussey, and to the correspondence between her
and Charlotte, for distinct and circumstantial accounts of life in the Parsonage in the
three years succeeding Charlotte's gradua-
tion from Roe Head. In parting, the friends

had engaged to exchange letters regularly every month. Mrs. Gaskell was painfully impressed, she says, with Charlotte's lack of hopefulness. When pleasure came she invariably met it with surprise, often mingled with incredulity. "Too good to be true," was the language of thought, if not always of tongue. Sorrow, pain, disappointment, were familiar guests, received without complaint, and given the liberty of heart and home. We descry a touch of this in the opening sentences of the first of the many letters, treasured for forty years by true-hearted, steadfast Ellen.

"HAWORTH, July 21, 1832.

"MY DEAREST ELLEN:

"Your kind and interesting letter gave me the sincerest pleasure. I have been expecting to hear from you almost every day since my arrival at home, and I, at length, began to despair of receiving the wished-for letter.

"You ask me to give you a description of the manner in which I have passed every day since I left school. This is soon done, as an account of one day is an account of all. In the mornings, from nine o'clock to half-past twelve, I instruct my sisters and draw ; then we walk 'till dinner. After dinner I sew 'till tea-time, and after tea I either read, write, do a little fancy-work, or draw, as I please. Thus, in one delightful, 'though somewhat monotonous course, my life is passed.   I have only been out to tea twice since I came home.   We are expecting company this afternoon, and on Tuesday next we shall have all the female teachers of the Sunday-school to tea.

"I do hope, my dearest Ellen, that you will return to school again for your own sake, 'though for mine I would rather that you would remain at home, as we shall then have more frequent opportunities of correspondence with each other.   Should your friends decide against your returning to school, I know you have too much good sense and right feeling not to strive earnestly for your own improvement.   Your natural abilities are excellent, and under the direction of a judicious and able friend (and I know you have many such) you might acquire a decided taste for elegant literature, and, even, poetry, which, indeed, is included under that general term.

"I was very much disappointed by your not sending the hair.   You may be sure, my dearest Ellen, that I would not grudge double postage to obtain it, but I must offer the same excuse for not sending you any.   My aunt and sisters desire their love to you.   Remember me kindly to your mother and sisters, and accept all the fondest expressions of genuine attachment from your real friend,                    " CHARLOTTE BRONTË.

" P. S.—Remember the mutual promise we made of a regular correspondence with each other.   Excuse all faults in this wretched scrawl.   Give my love to the Miss Taylors when you see them.

"Farewell, my *dear, dear, dear* Ellen ! " *

The smile tempted by the prim, elder-sisterly advice-giving gives way to a sigh

* Shorter's *Charlotte Brontë and Her Circle*, page 77.

as the passionate heart speaks out in the last line of the postscript. It was never easy for her to unveil the throbbing depths even to those she loved most fondly.

"She needed her best spirits to say what was in her heart," writes Mary Taylor ("Rose Yorke").

Mary's first visit to the wilds of Haworth made her acquainted with the aunt of whom Charlotte never talked to her schoolfellows, while ready to speak of her father and sisters, and to expatiate upon her brother's talents. Miss Taylor's conversations with the admirable spinster may have haunted Charlotte while she wrote of "Rose Yorke's" vehement protest against her mother's domestic training:

"If my Master has given me ten talents, my duty is to trade with them and make them ten talents more. Not in the dust of household drawers shall the coin be interred. I will *not* deposit it in a broken-spouted tea-pot and shut it up in a china-closet among tea-things. I will *not* commit it to your work-table to be smothered in piles of oollen whose. I will *not* prison it in the linen-press to find shrouds among the sheets. Least of all, will I hide it in a tureen of cold potatoes, to be ranged with bread, butter, pastry, and ham, on the shelves of the larder.

"Mother! the Lord Who gave each of us our talents

will come home some day, and will demand from all an account. Suffer your daughters, at least, to put their money to the exchangers, that they may be enabled at the Master's coming, to pay Him His own with usury."

"She made her nieces sew with purpose, and without," writes Miss Taylor, "and, as far as possible, discouraged any other culture. She used to keep the girls sewing on charity clothing, and maintained to me that it was not for the good of the recipients, but of the sewers. 'It was proper for them to do it,' she said."

There is meaning, and much of it, in the words, "she maintained to me." The independent girl of advanced ideas must have had more than one passage-at-arms with a spinster of the old school, resolute in the refusal to see any good in "views and innovations." Ellen Nussey ingratiated herself with the unbending mentor of fancies and follies at her first visit to Haworth. Charlotte's letter to her dearest friend, written just after the latter had returned home, has a joyous bound of spirits unusual in her speech or correspondence. Mary's experience with her aunt may have made her nervous as to the effect Ellen might produce.

"Papa and aunt are continually adducing you as an example for me to shape my actions and behaviour by," she says, gaily. "Emily and Anne say 'they never

HAWORTH PARSONAGE BEFORE IT WAS ALTERED

saw anyone they liked so well as you.' And Tabby,
whom you have fascinated, talks a great deal more non-
sense about your ladyship than I care to repeat."

Uneventful though they were, a grey
dead level of prosaic living that would have
been intolerable to one used to town or
gay country society, I think those three
years—when Charlotte Brontë taught her
sisters, sewed dutifully under her aunt's
direction, and found, according to her own
statement, "the two great pleasures and
relaxations of her day" in drawing and
walks up the heathery slopes of the moors
—were the serenest period of her life.

" My home is humble and unattractive to strangers,
but to me it contains what I shall find nowhere else in
the world,—the profound, the intense affection which
brothers and sisters feel for each other when their minds
are cast in the same mould, their ideas drawn from the
same source ; when they have clung to each other from
childhood, and when disputes have never sprung up to
divide them."

Thus she wrote out of the fulness of an
aching heart when the happy home party
was broken up by events that projected a
shadow over the year 1834-5.

I use the word "shadow" mindfully, for
at this turning of her life, the figure of her

brother is brought, for the first time, boldly into the foreground. He was next to her in age, being now nearly eighteen, but a year younger than Charlotte and a year older than Emily. Had the whole family entered into a league and covenant to spoil the only boy, the evil work could not have been more thoroughly done. Charlotte's letters show that she had her full share, perhaps more than any of the others, in puffing him up with conceit of his talents, and, as an inevitable *sequitur* with a weak, vain, passionate, provincial lad, inoculating him with a despicable contempt for the women of the household, and tolerant patronage of his father. Mr. Brontë taught his son Latin, Greek, and mathematics in the same antiquated manner in which the daughters were instructed. Other education he had none beyond what he got at the Haworth Grammar School, and picked up in the Parsonage study and at the indifferent circulating library in the neighbourhood. Like his sisters, he wrote poems, tales, tragedies, and essays, took lessons in drawing, and practised what of the art he had acquired. One and all, they thought him handsome. Charlotte speaks of his

" noble face and forehead," and says that
" Nature favoured him with a fairer outside, as well as a fairer constitution, than
his sisters." Not one of his adoring kinspeople doubted his genius. It is enigmati-
cal to the critic of the vapid verse, the turgid
tragedies, the trite prose, treasured by himself, and after his death by his sisters, how
even love could have been so pitiably
deceived.

" The clever one of the family," is the
verdict of townspeople, dazzled by the tin-
sel of what Charlotte's "cleverality" fitly
denotes. Superficial and flashy in conversation, he was undeniably heavy with the
pen. In the persuasion that his talents
needed but to be known to be appreciated
by the public at large, he sought sponsor-
ship from Coleridge and Wordsworth,
receiving small encouragement from either.
It would have been strange had any other
result followed the perusal of such lines as

> " I 'll lay me down on this marble stone
>    And set the world aside,
>   To see upon her ebon throne
>    The Moon in glory ride."

Charlotte and Emily were of the " half-
a-dozen people in the world " who, as

Branwell informs Wordsworth, "knew that he had ever penned a line." Charlotte's fond faith in his abilities had sustained no jar when the question came up in the family council — "What shall we do with our Genius ?"

Other reasons besides his eighteen years and bourgeoning talents moved father and aunt to the opinion that the youth should be set to work, and without delay. The Black Bull, a picturesque and ancient hostelry, stands just below the church steps, and within one minute's sharp run from the gate of the Parsonage. For two hundred and fifty years the tap-room has been the resort of the social and the thirsty among the Haworth folk, and for the same time the succession of landlordship has been from father to son in one line. Worthy, respectable men, all of them, who kept as decent and well-ordered a house as any in Yorkshire, or in England. There was conviviality, but not dissipation, in the gathering, on Saturday nights and other leisure evenings, of honest cottagers and millhands about the long oaken table embrowned by a century's usage, and indented by the heels of innumerable pew-

ter flagons. The home-brew of the Black
Bull deserves a reputation that has become
international in the last fifty years. The
most constant *habitué* of the venerable inn
was seldom the worse for what he had im-
bibed, however long the sitting. Mine
host saw to it that the house was cleared
at a reasonable hour, and never allowed
brawling, however large and promiscuous
the company.

The company was never so well pleased
as when Branwell Brontë—"Patrick" to
his hail-fellow-well-met townsmen—sat in
the triangular chair in the warmest corner
of the inn parlour, and told stories and
cracked jokes for the delectation of the
wondering revellers. To the simple souls
he was a miracle of learning and wit. They
extolled him at home, in the mill, in the
market-place, as the prodigy of the region.
When strangers from Bradford, Leeds, or
London passed a night at the Black Bull,
a messenger was despatched to the Parsonage for the "young maister," who, nothing
loath, as may be imagined, took upon his
facile self the entertainment of the traveller,
and exerted himself to live up to his reputation.

A stock story in the Black Bull *répertoire* is how one evening Charlotte's voice was heard at the front door asking if her brother were there ; whereupon the boy ran into the adjoining kitchen and jumped out of a window into the yard.  Some one went forward to meet the young lady, sobering his face to reply that "Patrick" was not in the house.  When telegraphed that the coast was clear, Branwell climbed in at the window and made his bow laughingly to the applauding crowd.  They thought it no harm to hoodwink the anxious sister. The boy was doing no wrong, and "it wor main dull at th' Parsonage for a loively lad."

It *was* dull for him, or for any young person who craved society or other amusement than books.  The girls wrote or studied all the evening in the parlour.  On the other side of the hall, Mr. Brontë was busy in his way, and must not be interrupted.  Miss Branwell retired early ; even the kitchen was deserted and dark.  In the profound stillness the ticking of the clock on the stairs could be heard all over the house.  Nobody called, and nothing ever happened.  A pot-house audience was

preferable to none; the adulation of the
illiterate tickled a palate not naturally over-
delicate. Such ignoble adventures as stealing out of the side door, racing down the
short lane, and leaping into the midst of
the ale-bibbers and smokers with some racy
epigram or saucy salutation, when father
and sisters thought him asleep in his room
above-stairs, quickened young blood and
hurt nobody.

Mr. Brontë was of yeoman stock, and at
no time held himself offensively aloof from
his parishioners. Nevertheless, he was not
insensible to the danger that his weaker son
ran in his present associations, and lent a
willing ear to the proposal brought forward
by Charlotte, Emily, and Anne, that the promising brother should go to London, be enrolled as a pupil in the Royal Academy of
Art, and forthwith set about the accomplishment of the foregone conclusion of becoming famous. We catch contagious
enthusiasm from Charlotte's announcement
of the great scheme to Ellen Nussey:

" We are all about to divide, break up, separate. Emily
is going to school, Branwell is going to London, and I am
going to be a governess! This last determination I formed
myself, knowing that I should have to take the step

sometime, and ' better sune as syne,' to use the Scotch proverb ; and knowing well that Papa would have enough to do with his limited income, should Branwell be placed at the Royal Academy, and Emily at Roe Head.

" Where am I going to reside ? you will ask. Within four miles of you, at a place neither of us is unacquainted with, being no other than the identical Roe Head mentioned above. Yes ! I am going to teach in the very school where I was myself taught. Miss Wooler made me the offer, and I preferred it to one or two proposals of private governess-ship which I had before received. I am sad—very sad—at the thought of leaving home ; but duty—necessity—these are stern mistresses, who will not be disobeyed.

" Did I not once say you ought to be thankful for your independence ? I felt what I said at the time, and I repeat it now with double earnestness. If anything would cheer me, it is the idea of being so near you. Surely, you and Polly will come and see me ; it would be wrong in me to doubt it ; you were never unkind yet. Emily and I leave home on the 27th of this month [July]. The idea of being together consoles us both somewhat, and, truth, since I must enter a situation, ' My lines have fallen in pleasant places.' I both love and respect Miss Wooler."

# CHAPTER VIII

### EMILY BRONTË—CHARLOTTE'S GOVERNESS-SHIP

UP to the date of Charlotte Brontë's governess-ship at Roe Head, her sister Emily is as little conspicuous in the household group as Anne—"gentle and loving," to borrow Sarah De Garrs's words, "acknowledging her sisters as her superiors in all things."

With this, her second absence from home, certain peculiarities of Emily's become evident and pronounced. Mary Taylor had seen in her a slim, long-limbed girl, taller than her sisters, and so reserved as to appear repellent. Mrs. Gaskell draws a just distinction between her reserve and Anne's shyness:

"Shyness would please, if it knew how. Reserve is indifferent whether it pleases or not."

It is well known that Emily was Charlotte's best-belovèd sister. Shirley was the writer's ideal of "what Emily Brontë would have been, had she been placed in health and prosperity."

No visitor who is now admitted to Haworth Rectory fails to pause to look at the narrow well at the foot of the crooked staircase leading from first to second storey. Keeper—the bulldog Tartar of *Shirley*—was Emily's guard abroad and familiar at home.

"A blow is what he is not used to, and will not take!" exclaims Shirley, as the Irish curate raises his cane against the "black-muzzled, tawny dog."

The gift of Keeper to Emily was coupled with a like warning.

"He is peaceable enough unless he is struck. Then he is dangerous," said the former owner. Emily was on such good terms with all her dumb pets—cats, chickens, and dogs—that the big, faithful fellow was long with her before the trial-day for both came. His one bad habit was to jump upon the most comfortable bed he could find, for his daily siésta, a trick of which neither scolding nor argument could break him. When discovered at last by Tabby in the middle of the bed in the guest-chamber, Emily engaged to punish him as he deserved. Without a word, she marched straight to the room, seized the culprit by the loose skin on the back of his neck, and dragged him down the steps, he growling all the way and pulling back with all his might. At the foot of the staircase she pushed him hard into the narrow nook behind the newel-post, and beat him on the head and jaws with her clenched fist until he cowered, conquered, at her feet.

Charlotte told the rest of the story, altering scene and names:

" She had not a word for anybody else during the rest of the day ; but sat near the hall-fire till evening, watching and tending Tartar, who lay all gory, stiff, and swelled, on a mat at her feet. She wept furtively over him sometimes, and murmured the softest words of pity and endearment, in tones whose music the old, scarred, canine warrior acknowledged by licking her hand, or her sandal, alternately with his own red wounds."

Emily's love of dogs had nearly proved fatal to her at one time, and this accident, also, Charlotte incorporated in *Shirley*.

Standing at the kitchen door, opening upon the lane, Emily saw a tramp cur trotting toward her, panting hoarsely, his tongue lolling low and long from his jaws. Supposing that he was suffering from the heat of the day, she ran back into the kitchen for a pail of water, and carried it out to him. In setting it down, she offered to pat his head, speaking soothingly to him. Instead of drinking, the brute snapped at her bare arm, drawing the blood with his teeth, then ran madly down the street.

Emily had left the ironing-board to look out of the door. Without calling for help, she went back into the kitchen, and snatched the hottest iron from the fire, a slender rod used in crimping. The tip was a clear scarlet ; she bored it well into the little wounds, drew down her sleeve over the scarified spot, and did not speak of it, even to Charlotte, until nine days had passed, and she thought the danger over.

Charlotte was reticent unless when moved to expression by deep feeling. Emily was always taciturn. Her sisters understood her in her dumbest moods. She did not care who else misapprehended her. It is marvellous how little is known of her personal traits and habits, with all the keen research instigated by admiration of the rare genius displayed in her one published book, *Wuthering Heights*. If she wrote letters they were not preserved by the recipients; she had no intimates except her sisters and, until his fall, her brother. A friend, who had seen as much of her as anyone not of her name and blood, told Mrs. Gaskell that " she never showed regard to any human creature. All her love was reserved for animals."

At Cowan Bridge she was the youngest pupil, and petted by the school. I fancy that this was her only experience of such fondling and indulgence as would rightfully fall to the lot of a pretty five-year-old girl in such circumstances.

Sarah De Garrs says of her at that age: "She was the only one of the children who ever required a hint as to forgotten bootlaces, or a soiled pinafore, and then only when there was an interesting book in the way." Of her as a woman, the same attached friend asks, "How can I describe the master-spirit of the talented trio? Will her character ever be fully apprehended?"

Her humble neighbours knew her by

sight, of course, but those who survive have less to tell than of the others. " She kept herself much to herself, and had little to say to anybody,"—sums up their reminiscences. One told me that "some thought her the prettiest of the girls." For his part, he "did not call her handsome, but she was, so to speak, ' high-looking.'" In a company exceeding in number Charlotte's two or three friends, whose repeated visits accustomed the inmates of the house to their presence, Emily was awkward and constrained, making no effort to put others, or herself, at ease. On the moors—her head up and nostrils dilated, like a deer-hound that scents the game, her dogs at her heels—her step was free and swift, her carriage graceful. Thus Charlotte saw her in the mirror of her mind when she begins a letter to her, " Mine own bonnie love."

With all her love of nature and outdoor life, she was, *par excellence*, the niece whose housewifely skill did most·honour to Miss Branwell's training. She did all the ironing, and most of the baking, besides bearing an important part in such scenes as Charlotte reviews in another letter to her favourite sister :

"I should like uncommonly to be in the dining-room at home, or in the kitchen, or in the back kitchen. I should like even to be cutting up the hash, and you standing by, watching that I put enough flour, not too much pepper, and, above all, that I save the best pieces of the leg of mutton for Tiger and Keeper, the first of which personages would be jumping about the dish and carving-knife, and the latter standing like a devouring flame on the kitchen floor. To complete the picture, Tabby blowing the fire in order to boil the potatoes to a sort of vegetable glue. How divine are these recollections to me at this moment!"

"Emily is going to school!"—Charlotte had said it jubilantly, and spoken hopefully of the comfort they would be to one another at Roe Head. At the close of the first quarter, the elder sister wrote urgently to her father to lay his commands upon Emily to return to Haworth. The eagle pined in the poultry-yard. From the first day of text-books, classes, and schoolroom hours, the girl was appetiteless and haggard; homesickness in its worst form seized upon her. Ashamed of the weakness, she threw herself furiously upon her studies,—wrought at the novel tasks as for her life. Charlotte tells with what result:

"In this struggle her health was quickly broken. Her white face, attenuated form, and failing strength threatened rapid decline. Her nature proved too strong for her fortitude."

Back at home, with the great, unbroken hollow of the sky above her, the wind from twenty miles of treeless moorland in her face, she rallied quickly, and tried to atone for the failure to secure such an education as other young women of her station received. The line of study prescribed at school was pursued indefatigably. She conned her German grammar while she kneaded the dough for the semi-weekly baking, the book propped up before her, out of reach of flour-dust or spatter of yeast. Whatever her employment, a book was ever within reach. How well she succeeded in equipping the ardent intellect discriminating critics never weary of telling.

Branwell was again in Haworth almost as soon as Emily. For some mysterious reason he did not enter the Royal Academy. Either the specimens of his work exhibited to the committee of inspection were unsatisfactory, or, as is generally suspected, he squandered the stipend allowed him by his father, and Mr. Brontë cut off further supplies. He would probably have thrown

himself away had he stayed in London
and been set to work at the art he loved,
or believed that he loved. Moral and physical ruin was made certain by the life he led
as gentleman-at-large in Haworth, painting
when he felt like it, carousing at the Black
Bull, writing rhymes by the ream, and gun-
ning on the moors with the sons of small
squires and mill-owners.

But for the solicitude on his account that
could not but steal over her spirits as news
of his idleness reached her, Charlotte would
have been as peacefully contented at Roe
Head as she could be anywhere away from
Haworth. Ellen Nussey's home, "Brookroyd," was within walking distance, as was
the Taylors', and Miss Wooler's thoughtful
kindness made frequent intercourse a pleasant possibility. We hear of Sundays spent
with both families ; of parcels tossed over
the wall on Huddersfield Market-day as
one of the Nussey or Taylor brothers
"whirled past" the enclosed playground
in sight of Charlotte's window. Her duties
were not onerous ; her pupils liked her and
studied satisfactorily ; she had the affectionate confidence of her employer, and her
moderate salary clothed herself and Anne.

Ellen Nussey paid a visit to the Parsonage during the midsummer holidays ; there were long summer afternoons among the heathery hills, then in their beautiful garments of royal purple, and merry evenings in the home parlour, and, thanks to the gentle magic of the guest's tact, many really natural girlish confidences ;—and the weeks of relaxation were flown. Ellen went home, Charlotte to begin the term of 1836–37 with Miss Wooler.

Branwell had set up a studio, without waiting for further instruction, and was painting portraits, sometimes going to Bradford to wait upon sitters. If those in the Brontë Museum at Haworth are fair specimens of his work, it is astonishing that he ever obtained a second order after the first picture was completed. They are sixteenth-rate as to execution, tasteless as to conception and style.

An important change in its consequences to Charlotte was made by Miss Wooler in 1836. She removed her school to Dewsbury Moor, a handsome building three miles from cozy Roe Head, and upon much lower ground. Miasma, or some kindred evil, told almost immediately upon Charlotte's health and spirits. She had darkly morbid fancies, confided partially to Ellen, whose "mild, steady friendship consoled her, however bitterly she sometimes felt toward other people." Emily had made another desperate effort to conquer nature in taking a place as pupil-teacher in a Halifax school, and the " appalling account " Charlotte received of her duties there added to the elder sister's depression.

"Hard labour from six in the morning to eleven at night, with only one half-hour of exercise between. This is *slavery !* I fear she can never stand it."

A long breathing-spell blessed them at Christmas ; a holiday made memorable, we are told by Mrs. Gaskell, by an exchange of confidences on the part of the sisters with respect to plans they had formed and fostered of publishing some of the many things they had written. At this date we have also the first mention of a custom kept up by the sisters as long as life lasted for each of them. Their aunt went to her room at nine o'clock, leaving the girls at liberty to spend the rest of the evening as they pleased. Even then the methodical habits drilled into them from their birth prevailed above inclination. They studied, or wrote, or sewed until the hall-clock struck ten, before work was put aside. If the fire in the pinched grate, but half the size of that which now fills its place, were low, they left a candle burning upon the table. If there were firelight enough to show the dim outlines of furniture and figures, they put out the candles "for economy's sake," and locking arms, paced around the room, up and down, backward and forward, while pouring out their hearts to one another. I think the half-light would have been preferred to illumination had frugality been less expedient. Reserve was strong second nature by now, and confidences were impracticable, even with those they loved best, when eyes searched the speaker's face, and changing expression was the thermometer of emotion.

People who met Charlotte as a celebrity speak of her way of turning away from her interlocutor as she talked, gradually shifting her position until she sat sideways in her chair, a mannerism due to early seclusion and attendant bashfulness.

The friendly glooms of the quiet parlour

favoured free discussion of past failures, present perplexities, and the possibilities of the future. Charlotte and Emily were governesses because there was no other way open by which they could earn a living ; Anne was to go back with Charlotte to Miss Wooler's as a pupil, to prepare for the same profession—hateful to all three, to Emily insupportable. They detested teaching ; they loved to write. With each the pen was a fuller outlet of feeling and thought than the tongue ; the Open Sesame to the wide, beautiful world of " things not seen " they had made for themselves as a retreat from, and a solace for, the narrow sordidness of visible and temporal things. At the suggestion that they might live by, as well as in, the exercise of the gifts they acknowledged to themselves and to each other, their souls took fire. In the audacity of their excitement they resolved to take the first great step in the road they, in their unworldliness, conceived would lead to success. Charlotte was commissioned to ask counsel of the Poet Laureate, Robert Southey. He had climbed the heights and could tell them whether or not they might adventure hill and pass. They knew him by reputation to be gentle of heart and kindly of disposition. He would condescend to tyros of low estate.

The momentous letter, so carefully prepared as to seem stilted to the verge of bombast, was despatched on the twenty-ninth of December, 1836.

Emily had been slaving beyond her strength in the Halifax school ; Charlotte bearing with what patience will and religion gave her the sickness of hope deferred, while teaching the youngest girls at Miss Wooler's ; Anne's timid sweetness had made friends of teachers and scholars—when, early in March, Mr. Southey's answer was forwarded from Haworth to Dewsbury Moor.

It was kind, it was sensible,—from the standpoint of a disinterested critic who knew nothing of his correspondent beyond what her letter told him,—and it was frank. Absence from home had delayed his letter. Nor was it " an easy task to answer it, nor a pleasant one to cast a damp over the high spirits and the generous desires of youth."

(Poor Charlotte ! did the wording of the merciful preamble smite her as a bitter irony ?)

The Laureate prosed on platitudinally,
with faint praise of the verses she had enclosed, with warnings as to the peril of
day-dreams and romantic expectations,
until he reached the pith of the communication.

" Literature cannot be the business of a woman's life,
and it ought not to be.  The more she is engaged in her
proper duties, the less leisure will she have for it, even as
an accomplishment and a recreation.  To those duties
you have not yet been called, and when you are, you
will be less eager for celebrity.  You will not seek in
imagination for excitement, of which the vicissitudes of
this life, and the anxieties from which you must not
hope to be exempted, be your state what it may, will
bring with them but too much.  .  .  .
" Write poetry for its own sake—not in a spirit of
emulation, and not with a view to celebrity.  The less
you aim at that, the more likely you will be to deserve,
and finally to attain it.  So written it is wholesome,
both for the heart and soul.  It may be made the surest
means, next to Religion, of soothing the mind and
elevating it.  You may embody in it your best thoughts
and your wisest feelings, and, in so doing, discipline and
strengthen them."

When the logic of events—often ruthless,
sometimes, thank Heaven! gracious and
compensatory—had proved the worthless-
ness of the great one's advice, Charlotte said

of his letter: "It was kind and admirable. A little stringent, but it did me good."

I wish a just sense of the proportions to be observed in this biography warranted the insertion of every line of her reply to the death-knell of her fondest hopes and happiest aspirations. I cannot deny my reader the perusal, and myself a repetition, of a part of it:

"At the first perusal of your letter, I felt only shame and regret that I had ever ventured to trouble you with my crude rhapsody. I felt a painful heat rise to my face when I thought of the quires of paper I had covered with what once gave me so much delight, but which now was only a source of confusion. But after I had thought a little, and read it again and again, the prospect seemed to clear. You do not forbid me to write ; you do not say that what I write is utterly destitute of merit. You only warn me against the folly of neglecting real duties for the sake of imaginative pleasures. You kindly allow me to write poetry for its own sake, provided I leave undone nothing which I ought to do, in order to pursue that single, absorbing, exquisite gratification. . . .

"I trust I shall never more feel ambitious to see my name in print. If the wish should rise, I 'll look at Southey's letter and suppress it. It is honour enough for me that I have written to him, and received an answer. That letter is consecrated. No one shall ever see it, but Papa and my brother and sisters. Again, I thank you ! This incident, I suppose, will be renewed no more. If

I live to be an old woman, I shall remember it, thirty years hence, as a bright dream."

In this remarkable epistle—the English of which is stronger than Southey could have written, while the spirit has the grave simplicity of a child—the woman and daughter put herself upon record.

Southey was so much touched by it that he wrote again, inviting her to visit him should she ever find herself in his neighbourhood, and counselling her to avoid over-excitement, and to keep a quiet mind. "Your moral and spiritual improvement will then keep pace with the culture of your intellectual powers."

Humane and patronising moralist! Let us be glad, for his sake, that he never suspected what flinty particles were kneaded up in the comely loaf he bestowed upon a half-starved soul.

# CHAPTER IX

## DEWSBURY MOOR—FIRST OFFER OF MARRIAGE

EMILY remained in Halifax half a year, a period of exquisite suffering borne dumbly and without a struggle. Finally her health succumbed to the strain, and the fiat went forth. She must go back to Haworth if she would not be permanently invalided. There was work in abundance for her there. Tabby had had a serious accident that lamed her for life, and Miss Branwell was growing old. Branwell was painting, idling, and drinking. Anne was still at school, and Charlotte was the only breadwinner besides her father. In spite of the (to her) unsalubrious air of Dewsbury Moor, she stood valiantly at her post for two years, keeping her word to Mr. Southey and seeking, in conscientious performance of "her proper duties," to dull the ceaseless longing to be something more than an automaton, to do something higher than mix and administer mental pap for babes.

In mid-May of 1838, the month when bird-songs were sweetest and the springing heather at its tenderest green on the dear moors, Miss Wooler insisted upon calling in medical advice for her young assistant. The girl's nerves—not her nerve —were giving out. She was semi-hysterical after the day's work was done; she was a prey to insomnia; she could not eat. The physician spoke plainly to Miss Wooler. Miss Brontë's life and reason were in danger. She was fairly worn out. In modern technical phrase, she was on the verge of nervous prostration. But one thing could save her. She must have rest and change, and these in the breezy uplands for which she pined.

In June she wrote to Ellen Nussey of dawning convalescence:

" A calm and even mind like yours cannot conceive the feelings of the shattered wretch who is now writing to you when, after weeks of mental and bodily anguish not to be described, something like peace began to dawn again. My health and spirits had utterly failed me, and the medical man whom I consulted, enjoined me, as I valued my life, to go home."

At Mr. Brontë's earnest invitation, the two Taylor sisters paid a visit to their friend the first week in June. Mary was not well, but Martha "kept up a continual flow of good humour during her stay, and has, consequently, been very fascinating."

The brightest picture we have of Haworth home life is given in this letter written in the family sitting-room. Mary Taylor is, Charlotte says, at the piano ; Martha, vivacious, piquante, and restless, is talking animatedly to Branwell, as he stands before her, looking laughingly down into her face. We have no other view of the weak and facile son of the house half so pleasing as this.

It must have been during this tranquil year spent by all three sisters at home, except for Charlotte's occasional visits to the Nusseys and Taylors, that the picture was painted of which I secured a rough photograph in Haworth. I was there assured that the original was painted by Branwell Brontë, although no mention is made of it by that most careful of the Brontë chroniclers, Professor Clement Shorter. The

workmanship is atrocious, but people who
knew the family say the likenesses are so far
worthy of the name that they can be iden-
tified.    Charlotte  sits  at  her  brother's
right hand, Emily next to her, and Anne
alone at the other end of the table.    Branwell's sporting propensities are characteris-
tically indicated by the fowling-piece and
game.  His social ambitions lay in the direction of the country gentleman, and these
tastes were not lessened by the poor emin-
ence  accorded  him  by  the  illiterate  con-
stituency of the tap-room.

A worthy Thornton shoemaker, formerly
a  resident  of  Haworth,  and  who  made
shoes for the Brontës as long as he lived
there, told me an anecdote illustrative of
the flashiness the weak young fellow mis-
took for dash:

" He would be about eighteen when I made him the
boots I mind of.    Most folk, at that day, had boots
made to coom up to the knee—some above the knee.
Top-boots, you know.    Patrick Brontë would have his
lower to wear with gaiters for hunting on the moors,
and the like.    I made the pair, and when he put thim
on, they wor a bit toight in the instep and aboot th'
ankle.    And, with that, before I could say a word to
tell him I 'd stretch thim, he whipped oot his jack-knife
and cut thim open.    Ah ! he wor a rare one ! "

Plain common-sense reminds us that a lad who was not earning enough to pay his board, and whose father was growing old and had three daughters to be provided for, was inhuman, as well as extravagant, in slashing into what his father must pay for. The reckless bit of folly fastened the incident in the shoemaker's mind, and the air with which it was done moved him to admiration rather than reprobation.

Branwell and Emily were left at home when gentle Anne took a place as governess in April, 1839, and Charlotte entered the family of Mr. Sidgwick, a wealthy country gentleman at Stonegappe, Yorkshire.

Anne's experience is condensed into one sentence in a confidential letter from Charlotte to Ellen Nussey: "*You* could never live in an unruly, violent family of children such as those at Ingham Hall."

Her own engagement was temporary, to fill the place of the regular governess, who had leave of absence for three months. Charlotte congratulated herself upon this circumstance after a short trial of the situation. Her employer was a hard, haughty *parvenue,* who "overwhelmed her with oceans of needlework, yards of cambric to

BRONTË GROUP

FROM A PAINTING BY BRANWELL BRONTË

hem, muslin night-caps to make, and dolls to dress."

"I see now, more clearly than I have ever done before, that a private governess has no existence, is not considered as a living, and rational, being except as connected with the wearisome duties she has to fulfil," she breaks out bitterly. A significant caution follows in the latter part of the letter: "Don't show this to Papa or Aunt, but *only to Branwell*. They will think I am never satisfied wherever I am. I complain to you because it is a relief, and really I have had some unexpected mortifications to put up with."

A week later she asks Ellen to

"imagine the miseries of a reserved wretch thrown at once into the midst of a large family, proud as peacocks and rich as Jews, at a time when they were particularly gay, when the house was filled with company — all strangers. . . .

"At first I was for giving up all and going home. But after a little reflection I said to myself,—'I had never quitted a place without gaining a friend ; adversity is a good school ; the poor are born to labour and the dependent to endure.' . . . I recollected the fable of the willow and the oak. I bent quietly, and now I trust the storm is blowing over. . . . I have no wish to be pitied except by yourself."

It was the mistress of this family who, when one of her children impulsively threw his arms about his teacher's neck with, "I *love* 'ou, Miss Brontë !" ejaculated reprovingly, "Fie ! love the *governess*, my dear !"

"The dreary 'gin-horse' round," as she calls governessing, may have been the more intolerable for an opportunity offered her, just before she accepted the proposal to go to the Sidgwicks, of escaping at once, and forever, from a life which she abhorred and dreaded.

Henry Nussey, a young clergyman, the brother of her dearest friend, asked her to marry him. The letter in which the declaration of his regard was made was, as she afterward told his sister, "written without cant or flattery, and in a common-sense style which does credit to his judgment."

With the looming horror of a "situation" before her, she answered the honourable gentleman she would retain as a friend, kindly and candidly:

"I have no personal repugnance to the idea of a union with you,' but I feel convinced that mine is not the sort of disposition calculated to form the happiness

of a man like you. . . . You do not know me. I
am not the serious, grave, cool-headed individual you
suppose. You would think me romantic and eccentric.
You would say I was satirical and severe. However, I
scorn deceit, and I will never, for the sake of attaining
the distinction of matrimony and escaping the stigma of
an old maid, take a worthy man whom I am conscious
I cannot render happy."

In this sisterly epistle she sketches what
manner of woman he ought to marry, evidently with a view to presenting a being
utterly antipodal to herself :

"Her character should not be too
marked, ardent, and original ; her temper
should be mild, her piety undoubted, her
spirits even and cheerful, and her *personal
attractions* sufficient to please your eyes
and gratify your just pride."

The italics are her own, and indicate
what was ever patent to her friends—an
exaggerated sense of her homely face and
ill-assured manner.

To Ellen, to whom her brother had confided his attachment and intended proposal,
Charlotte wrote yet more plainly:

"There were in this proposal some things which
might have proved a strong temptation. I thought if I
were to marry Henry Nussey his sister could live with
me, and how happy I should be. But again I asked

myself two questions : Do I love him as much as a woman ought to love the man she marries? Am I the woman best qualified to make him happy? Alas! Ellen, my conscience answered *no* to both those questions. I felt that, though I esteemed, though I had a kindly leaning toward him because he is an amiable and well-disposed man, yet I had not, and could not have, that intense attachment which would make me willing to die for him ; and, if ever I marry, it must be in that light of adoration that I will regard my husband.

"Ten to one I shall never have the chance again—but *n'importe!*

"Moreover, I was aware that Henry knew so little of me he could hardly be conscious to whom he was writing. Why, it would startle him to see me in my natural home-character. He would think I was a wild, romantic enthusiast indeed. I could not sit, all day long, making a grave face before my husband. I would laugh and satirise, and say whatever came into my head first. And, if he were a clever man and loved me, the whole world weighed in the balance against his smallest wish should be light as air. Could I, knowing my mind to be such as that, conscientiously say that I would take a grave, quiet young man like Henry? No! it would have been deceiving him, and deception of that sort is beneath me." *

Before leaving the subject of this, her first offer of marriage, it is well to state that in six months she was called upon to write a letter to Mr. Nussey, congratulatory upon his engagement to another woman, and that

* *Charlotte Brontë and Her Circle*, page 297.

he always remained her steadfast friend. She was a welcome guest at his house, and both parties to the quiet transaction in hearts seem to have been one in the desire to feel and act as if it had never ruffled the current of their intercourse.

In a very different strain she describes to Ellen a visit from a young Irish curate—

"witty, lively, ardent, clever, too, but deficient in the dignity and discretion of an Englishman. At home, you know, I talk with ease, and am never shy— never weighed down and oppressed by the miserable *mauvaise haute* which torments and constrains me else- where. So I conversed with this Irishman and laughed at his jests."

In effect she made herself so agreeable that she received by post a few days after his one and only visit

"a declaration of attachment and proposal of matri- mony, expressed in the ardent language of the sapient young Irishman.

"I hope you are laughing heartily ? This is not like one of my adventures, is it ? It more nearly resembles Martha's ["Jessie Yorke"]. I am certainly doomed to be an old maid. Never mind ! I made up my mind to that fate ever since I was twelve years old."

A letter bearing date of May 15, 1840, almost a year after she had dismissed her two suitors, fits in well here :

" Do not be over-persuaded to marry a man you can never respect—I do not say *love,* because I think if you can respect a person before marriage, moderate love, at least, will come after ; and as to intense passion, I am convinced that that is no desirable feeling.   In the first place it seldom, or never meets with a requital, and in the second place, if it did, the feeling would be only temporary.   It would last the honeymoon, and then, perhaps give place to disgust, or indifference—worse, perhaps, than disgust.   Certainly this would be the case on the man's part ;—and, on the woman's—God help her, if she is left to love passionately and alone !

" I am tolerably well convinced that I shall never marry at all.  Reason tells me so, and I am not so utterly the slave of feeling but that I can occasionally hear her voice."

The year had passed quietly, but neither idly nor unhappily.   Tabby's confirmed lameness obliged her to leave her situation and go to stay for a while with her sister. Charlotte and Emily did all the housework with no servant except a little errand-girl from the school in the lane near the Parsonage.  To Charlotte fell the chamber-work,— "blackleading the stoves, making the beds, and sweeping the floors,"—with the ironing. The first time she undertook the latter task she burned the clothes ; afterward she became an adept.  Emily was cook and baker.

"I am much happier than I should be living like a fine lady anywhere else," Charlotte affirmed. " Yet—I intend to force myself to take another situation when I can get one, though I *hate* and abhor the very thoughts of governess-ship. But I must do it, and therefore I heartily wish I could hear of a family where they need such a commodity as a governess."

The faultless system of housewifery learned from the aunt, and the simple habits of a family that had no visitors, left the sisters several hours of each day for writing and out-of-door exercise. In the winter of 1839–40 they conceived and discussed a scheme which, although it never took the shape they wished it to assume, was to exert a powerful influence upon their fortunes.

Anne was to be recalled, and the three sisters would open a home-school for girls in some eligible town not far from Haworth. The project formed the staple of the dialogues held in the parlour when the seniors were in bed, and the candles were extinguished to save expense, and the only sound in the old house besides the moaning wind and the ticking of the hall-clock was the soft, measured tread over the floor of the two whose restless shadows crossed the fire-lighted space about the pinched grate to blend with moveless shadows in the corners of the room. The cherished project promised so little that Charlotte was, all the while, on the lookout for another situation.

She wrote of a dim prospect of an engagement for herself, and of a certain opening for Branwell, late in the summer of 1840:

"A woman of the name of B——, it seems, wants a teacher. I wish she would have me, and I have written to Miss Wooler to tell her so. Verily, it is a delightful thing to live here at home, with full liberty to do just what one pleases. But I recollect some scrubby old fable about grasshoppers and ants by a scrubby old knave yclept Æsop. The grasshoppers sang all the summer, and starved all the winter.

"A distant relation of mine—one Patrick Branwell—has set off to seek his fortune in the wild, wandering, adventurous, romantic, knight-errant-like capacity of clerk on the Leeds and Manchester Railroad. Leeds and Manchester—where are they? Cities in the wilderness, like Tadmor, *alias* Palmyra—are they not?"

In the same letter we have a leaf from the record of Charlotte's parish-work and interesting incidents touching upon her association with her father's curates while thus engaged. Mr. Weightman, supposed by some to have been the suggestion of

little Mr. Sweeting, in *Shirley*, has given
her a pleasant surprise in the discovery of
his goodness to one of her Sunday-school
girls. Calling upon the girl, she

"found her on her way to that 'bourn whence no traveller returns,' and inquiry into her wants elicited the information that Mr. Weightman had provided delicacies
for the invalid and that he was 'always good-natured to
poor folks, and seemed to have a deal of feeling and
kind-heartedness about him.'

"God bless him!" breaks out Charlotte, impulsively,
repentant of sundry jests she and her sisters had passed
upon the natty little fellow. "I wonder who, with his
advantages, would be without his faults. I know many
of his faulty actions—many of his weak points; yet
where I am, he shall always find rather a defender than
accuser."

The admirer of "Shirley" as jaunty "Cap-
tain Keeldar" will like to know that Emily
Brontë earned the *sobriquet* of "Major" in
the family circle by guarding Ellen Nussey
from the attentions of "our revered friend,
William Weightman,"—so Charlotte rattles
on,—"who is quite as bonny, pleasant,
light-hearted, good-tempered, generous,
careless, fickle, and unclerical as ever." *

Mr. Bradley, a curate in another parish,

* *Charlotte Brontë and Her Circle*, page 287.

was thought by other friends of the Brontës to be the original of "Mr. Sweeting of Nunnely." Mr. Grant, sometime master of the Haworth Grammar School and Branwell's teacher, was "Mr. Donne." Of "Mr. Malone" we shall hear more, by-and-by.

# CHAPTER X

VARIOUS SCHOOL PROJECTS—"GOING TO BRUS-
SELS"—LIFE IN THE PENSIONNAT OF M. AND
MADAME HÉGER

"I AM, as yet, 'wanting a situation,' like
a housemaid out of place," Charlotte
had said in April, 1839. She did not obtain what she desired, yet "abhorred,"
until the spring of 1841. She had but two
pupils, both under ten years of age. Her
salary was twenty pounds a year, out of
which she was to pay all her expenses except board and lodging. The place, Up-
perwood House, Rawdon, the country-seat
of a Mr. White, was a decided improvement upon the temporary engagement with
the Sidgwicks. It is gratifying to have her
testimony to the kindness of her employers
in a letter to Henry Nussey, now resident
at Earnley Rectory, and a married man:

"We are all separated now, and winning our bread amongst strangers as we can. My sister Anne is near York, my brother in a situation near Halifax ; I am here. Emily is the only one left at home, where her usefulness and willingness make her indispensable. . . . I do not pretend to say that I am always contented. A governess must often submit to have the heartache. My employers, Mr. and Mrs. White, are kind, worthy people in their way, but the children are indulged. I have great difficulties to contend with sometimes. Perseverance will perhaps conquer them. And it has gratified me much to find that the parents are well satisfied with their children's improvement in learning since I came." *

The school project worked actively in her mind. Her father and aunt were consulted in the midsummer holidays of 1841, and did not throw cold water upon it, much to the sisters' surprise and gratification. Miss Branwell went so far as to promise to advance a hundred pounds for initial expenses should a good situation be secured. Burlington was thought of, and the claims of sundry other places were discussed in family council and by letter.

"No further steps have been taken about the project I mentioned to you," she told Ellen Nussey in August, "but Emily and Anne and I keep it in view. It is our polar star, and we look to it in all circumstances of

* *Charlotte Brontë and Her Circle,* page 88.

despondency. . . . You will not mention it at present. A project not actually commenced is always uncertain."

In this letter she speaks of Mary Taylor's having gone to Brussels with her brother, and of her descriptions of

" pictures the most exquisite, cathedrals the most venerable. I hardly know what swelled to my throat as I read her letter—such a strong wish for wings—*wings*, such as wealth can furnish ; such an urgent thirst to see, to know, to learn. Something internal seemed to expand bodily for a minute. I was tantalised by the consciousness of faculties unexercised ;—then, all collapsed and I *despaired !*

" My dear ! I would hardly make that confession to anyone but yourself, and to you, rather in a letter than *vivâ voce.*"

Another plan was uppermost in September and early October. Miss Wooler was giving up her school at Dewsbury Moor. Would the Brontës take it ? If they were disposed to do it, were their attainments in the matter of music and modern languages such as to warrant the belief that they could maintain the high tone of the seminary, and attract pupils of the better class ?

More abruptly than she was wont to address her best friend, Charlotte wrote, October 17, 1841 :

"I am not going to Dewsbury Moor, as far as I can
see at present. It was a decent, friendly proposal on
Miss Wooler's part ; but Dewsbury Moor is a poisoned
place to me.   Besides, I burn to go somewhere else.   I
think, Nell, I see a chance of getting to Brussels.   Mary
Taylor advises me to this step.   My own mind and
feelings urge me.   I can't write a word more."

The chance of having the wings for
which she had longed hopelessly, came in
the form of a loan from Miss Branwell,
whose annuity of fifty pounds had been
more than sufficient for her modest needs
during her residence at Haworth.   She had
husbanded her savings for her nieces, and
Charlotte, aware of this, boldly asked that
fifty, or perhaps one hundred, pounds be
laid out upon them now.   Emily was to
go with Charlotte to a Brussels school,
where

"the facilities for education are equal, or superior, to
any other place in Europe.
    "If Emily could share them with me, we could take
a footing in the world afterwards which we can never do
now.   I say, Emily, instead of Anne, for Anne might
take her turn at some future period if our school answered.
.   .   .   I feel an absolute conviction that, if this advantage were allowed us, it would be the making of us
for life."

The last sentence quoted was prophetic,
but the mill that brought it to pass ground

slowly, and the product was totally dissimilar to what the ambitious dreamer
scheduled to herself and her friends.

There is a joyous flutter of spirits in the
letter penned to Ellen in the last month
spent in England before the momentous
flitting :

" Mary has been indefatigable in providing me with
information. She has grudged no labour, and scarcely
any expense, to that end. Mary's price is above rubies.
I have, in fact, two friends—you and her—staunch and
true, in whose faith and sincerity I have as strong a belief as I have in the Bible. I have bothered you both,
you especially ; but you always get the tongs and heap
coals of fire upon my head. I have had letters to write
lately to Brussels, to Lille, and to London. I have lots
of chemises, night-gowns, pocket-handkerchiefs, and
pockets to make, besides clothes to repair. I have been,
every week, since I came home, expecting to see Branwell, and he has never been able to get over yet. We
fully expect him, however, next Saturday. Under these
circumstances, how can I go visiting? You tantalise me
to death, with talking of conversations by the fireside.
Depend upon it, we are not to have any such for many
a long month to come. I get an interesting impression
of old age upon my face, and when you see me next, I
shall certainly wear caps and spectacles." *

Mary Taylor and her brother (we wish
we knew whether it was " Mark " or

* Shorter's *Charlotte Brontë and Her Circle*, page 99.

"Martin") were returning to the Continent, and offered to take charge of the Brontë girls. Mr. Brontë insisted, nevertheless, upon escorting them in person. The party of five set out from Yorkshire the second week of February, 1842, spent a couple of days in London, then pushed on to Brussels. Mary and Martha Taylor were to study at the Château de Koekelberg, on the outskirts of the city. The Brontës had applied for admission at the Pensionnat of Monsieur and Madame Héger in Rue d'Isabelle, in the very heart of ancient Brussels.

The buildings occupied as a day- and boarding-school were old even then. The Rue d'Isabelle was an inhabited quarter in the thirteenth century. A broad flight of stone steps leads from the gay upper town to the quieter quarter. In descending these one sees directly opposite a long row of white houses, two and three storeys in height. Between the first and second *étages* of one of the taller is a sign denoting that an *école communale* (that is, a public school) is still kept here. What was the Hégers' private residence has been cut off from the school-buildings, and the garden in the rear of the hollow square of houses is built up in part.

The arrangement of the schoolrooms differs somewhat from that of 1842. The great *classe* has been cut into smaller reception-rooms, and the dormitories are disused, all the pupils in attendance upon the sessions of the school being *externes,* or day-scholars.

When the diligence deposited the Yorkshire clergyman and his daughters at the door bearing Madame Héger's name, there were a hundred girls and a large staff of teachers in the institution, and all the machinery of a successful fashionable seminary of polite learning was in full swing. Brussels is well named "a miniature Paris," and Madame Héger's patrons were, for the most part, prosperous citizens. Charlotte Brontë drew upon memory, not imagination, in depicting "Lucy Snowe's" surroundings and associates in *Villette.* The book is a marvel, less of creative genius than of descriptive art. Mr. Shorter says truly, "With a copy of *Villette* in hand it is possible to restore every feature of the place." The reader who knows *Villette* and *The Professor* needs no information respecting the external features of the place, and little as to Charlotte's ("Lucy's") employments and companions.

Let an **extract from** *The Professor* outline these last for such as have read neither novel:

" The majority belonged to the class *bourgeois ;* but there were many countesses, there were the daughters of two generals and of several colonels, captains, and government employés. These ladies sat side by side with young females destined to be *demoiselles de magasin,* and with some Flamandes, genuine aborigines of the country. In dress all were nearly similar, and in manners there was small difference. Exceptions there were to the general rule, but the majority gave the tone to the establishment, and that tone was rough, boisterous, marked by a point-blank disregard of all forbearance towards each other, or their teachers."

Neither book tells the piteous tale of the Brontë sisters' initiation into their new life. The rush and the bustle of shifting classes and of recitations; the stares of the well-dressed, well-fed girls herding together at recess to comment upon the late arrivals ; the shrill un-English voices chattering like maniacal parrots, in a jargon as unintelligible to Yorkshire ears as if the strangers had never "taken" a French lesson; the crowded table in the refectory ; the foreign cookery; the dormitory, furnished with ten beds on each side of a strait central aisle— were so many variations of pain and puzzle to Charlotte and Emily.   As a concession to English reserve, they were permitted to hang a curtain between their beds at the far end of the dormitory and the eighteen small white cots beyond.   When the school was turned out, like wild colts, into the garden behind the house for the noon exercise, the foreigners, older by eight or ten years than the eldest Belgian there, walked together and apart from the rest, in the vine-draped arbour (*berceau*) near the wall on the right of the grounds.

An odd-looking pair they were to friendly, as to curious, eyes.   Their dress, plain to singularity in Haworth, was *bizarre* and ridiculous in the petty Paris.   Long after they were discarded by everybody else, Emily clung to " mutton-leg " sleeves, full at the shoulder, baggy down to the elbow, and thence sloping abruptly to the wrist, where they fitted closely.   Her skirts were gathered at the belt and hung, straight, limp, and untrimmed, to the ankle.   No gores or flounces were tolerable in her eyes, let who would wear the fripperies.   Charlotte was indifferent to dress, yet Emily's biographer, Miss Robinson, more than hints at an effort on her part to conform her attire to prevailing modes. .

"She "—Emily—" would laugh when she found her elder sister trying to arrange her homely gowns in the French taste, and stalk silently through the large schoolrooms with a fierce satisfaction in her own ugly sleeves, in the Haworth cut of her skirts."

In this respect she was unlike the beautiful "Shirley." Emily despised all arts pertaining to personal adornment. Clothes were meant to cover the figure and to keep one warm. Beyond this she had no use for them. At rising in the morning she donned the gown she intended to wear all day, and dressed her hair with the like view. Arrayed as the loving sister makes Shirley bedeck herself on fête-days, Emily might have been comely. Miss Robinson, after the manner of other biographers, becomes her partisan before her fascinating task is half done. She paints Emily Brontë at home as

"a tall, lithe creature, with a grace, half queenly, half untamed, in her sudden, supple movements, wearing, with picturesque negligence, a white stuff patterned with lilac ' thunder and lightning ' ; her face clear and pale ; her very dark and plenteous brown hair fastened up behind with a Spanish comb."

To Madame Héger, her teachers, and her pupils, she was a dowdy, and *farouche* in behaviour. If she had comprehended the voluble French in which they exchanged witticisms upon her apparel and manners, she could not have been more obstinately taciturn. Her moods were almost as inclement with two other English girls in the foreign school. Charlotte, naturally and habitually shy, made friends. Emily remained a stranger to the last.

M. Héger, faithfully portrayed in *Villette* as "Paul Emmanuel," took especial interest in his Yorkshire students at an early date of their acquaintance. Charlotte speaks of him to Miss Nussey as "a man of power as to mind, but very choleric and irritable in temperament." In spicier phrase, she goes on :

"A little black being, with a face that varies in expression. Sometimes, he borrows the lineaments of an insane tom-cat ; sometimes, those of a delirious hyena. Occasionally, but very seldom, he discards these perilous attractions and assumes an air not above one hundred degrees removed from mild and gentlemanlike."

These first impressions were sensibly

modified as his hand opened to her avenues into the realm of knowledge and research for which her quickening intellect had pined through restless, hungry years. "We are completely isolated in the midst of numbers," she records. "Yet I think I am never unhappy. My present life is so delightful, so congenial to my whole nature, compared to that of a governess! My time, constantly occupied, passes too rapidly."

After the lively sketch of M. Héger already quoted, and an abstract of the method of instruction he had chosen for the sisters, she adds : "Emily and he don't draw together well at all. Emily works like a horse, and she has had great difficulties to contend with—far greater than I have had."

Yet the sagacious master adjudged Emily's to be the finer mind of the two. His expressed opinion was to the effect that "she should have been a man—a great navigator." Her reason was powerful, and in grasp sublime ; her turn for logical demonstration, phenomenal. There was no love lost between them ; French fire and English frost were antipathetic to the last, yet each did justice to the abilities of

the other.   The dogged energy with which
the proud, dumb girl wrought upon tasks
he could not make too arduous for her, or
for ambitious Charlotte, won his respect in
spite of his dislike of Emily's manner and
what he stormed at as obstinate adherence
to her own opinions, particularly when
these were backed up by her principles.

The winter slipped by more swiftly than
they could have believed possible in the
earlier weeks of homesickness and strange-
ness.   With the opening of the spring, the
garden was an habitual resort with the
pupils — " the strange, frolicsome, noisy
little world," in which the Brontës moved
without blending with the current of feeling and action.   As the days lengthened,

" the house became as merry a place as a school could
be.   All day long the broad folding doors and the two-
leaved casements stood wide open ; settled sunshine
seemed naturalised in the atmosphere. . . . We
lived far more in the garden than under a roof ; classes
were held, and meals partaken of in the ' grand *berceau*.' "

Charlotte had learned to speak and write
French with ease and grace, and, under
M. Héger's lead, the wings of her eager
mind had borne her far and high into re-
gions he never thought of tempting his

Belgian *élèves* to enter. Encouraged by him, she dared, not merely to think, but to analyse subjects and to define her independent conclusions.

Madame Héger was distrusted by the English girls under her charge, a sentiment of which one who herself trusted nobody, should not have complained. She was attractive in person, polished in manner, acute in mind, fluent in speech, a diplomate born, and endowed with extraordinary administrative genius. Her surveillance of school and household was incessant, and although deftly done, was a secret to none. The shoes of silence carried her into every classroom, every dormitory and closet under her roof, at all hours of day or night. Monsieur was irritable, fierce, unreasonable,—but he showed his hand in a fair game, and said his say in a wordy fight. Madame asked no questions when she could, by spying, find out all she wished to know ; she never scolded, and never lost her temper.

Madame Beck in *Villette* was Madame Héger to the life, and here we have Charlotte's masterly analysis of a character she read through to the last leaf :

"Madame was a very great, and a very capable woman. The school offered for her powers too limited a sphere. She ought to have swayed a nation ; she should have been the leader of a turbulent, legislative assembly. Nobody could have browbeaten her, none irritated her nerves, exhausted her patience, or over-reached her astuteness. In her own single person she could have comprised the duties of a first minister and a superintendent of police. Wise, firm, faithless ; secret, crafty, passionless ; watchful and inscrutable ; acute and insensate — withal, perfectly decorous — what more could be desired ? "

This woman it was who, as midsummer approached, proved her appreciation of the sterling qualities of the *drôle* English girls by offering to dismiss her English teacher and give his place to Charlotte Brontë, and to engage Emily as a pupil-teacher to assist a music-master. Intense application and the iron will that caused M. Héger to rage himself black in the face when opposed to his, had made Emily a brilliant pianist, with a thorough comprehension of the science of music as far as her studies had led her.

"The proposal is kind," writes Charlotte, "and implies a degree of interest which demands gratitude in turn. I don't deny I sometimes wish to be in England, or that I have brief attacks of homesickness, but on the whole, I have borne a very valiant heart thus far, and I have been happy in Brussels because I have been fully occupied with the employments that I like. Emily is making rapid progress in French, German, music, and drawing. Monsieur and Madame Héger begin to recognise the valuable parts of her character, under her singularities."

The proposal was accepted, and, instead of returning to England for the two months' vacation, the Brontës spent it in the almost deserted Pensionnat, hard at work. The only relief from the continuous strain was in the attendance at the school during the holidays, of four or five English girls, belonging to a family that had lately removed to Brussels. From one of these Mrs. Gaskell had a *résumé* that seems dreary to us of the routine duties incumbent upon the sisters in vacation and in the term succeeding it.

Their one hour of recreation on weekdays was spent in the garden. They walked in the trellised *berceau*, or in the *allée defendue*, a sequestered alley forbidden to the pupils because bounded on one side by the wall of the Athénée, a boys' college. The narrator notes that the pair rarely exchanged a word during these promenades. If met and addressed directly, Charlotte replied, always courteously and in a soft, even voice, Emily standing by, impassive and mute.  We do not wonder as we read, in close juxtaposition to this *résumé*, Mary Taylor's repetition of a remark made by Charlotte in one of her visits to the Château de Koekelberg :

"She seemed to think that most human beings were destined, by the pressure of worldly interests, to lose one faculty and feeling after another, till they went dead altogether.  'I hope I shall be put into my grave as soon as I 'm dead.  I don't want to walk about *so!* ' "

Martha Taylor ("Jessie Yorke") died in October, 1842, after a short illness.  Charlotte heard of her danger some hours before her death, and hastened to offer help and sympathy to Mary.  When she reached the Château it was to hear that the arch, engaging pet of Taylor and Brontë households had died in the night.

"I have seen Martha's grave," wrote Charlotte, mournfully,—"the place where her ashes lie in a foreign country."

The simple phrase is more pathetic than the much-quoted description in *Shirley* of Jessie's last resting-place.

Close upon this grief came news of Miss

Branwell's serious illness. Her nieces made haste to pack their trunks and engage places in the diligence for a hurried journey homeward. They were in the act of setting out when a second letter brought word that their aunt had died, October 29, 1842.

# CHAPTER XI

MISS BRANWELL'S WILL—SOME OF BRANWELL'S
FAILURES—CHARLOTTE'S SECOND YEAR IN
BRUSSELS—MONSIEUR HÉGER AND CHAR-
LOTTE BRONTË

WHILE living, Miss Elizabeth Branwell
had never been what the Italians
call *simpatica* with any of her nieces.
Anne, gentle and amiable, was decidedly
her favourite of the three. Her will proved
her to be both just and generous. All her
personal effects were to be divided equally
by Charlotte, Emily, and Anne, with the
exception of a "japan dressing-case"
which was to be given to Branwell. After
her just debts and the expenses of a "moderate and decent" funeral were paid, the
residue of her estate was to be invested in
"good landed security," or deposited "in
some safe bank," there to accumulate for

the benefit of her four nieces, the Brontë
girls and her namesake, Elizabeth Kings-
ton, in Penzance, until the youngest
legatee should attain the age of one-and-
twenty.   Then they were to share and
share alike.

I have already cited, in evidence of the
cordial relations existing between herself
and her brother-in-law, the fact that Mr.
Brontë was named first among her executors.

The will was written in 1833, nine years
before her decease, when Branwell—her
pet and pride—was in high favour.   Mr.
Shorter accounts for the small legacy left
to him by remarking, "The old lady
doubtless thought that the boy would be
able to take good care of himself."

As he assuredly should have been by
now.   His first essay in this direction was
in the capacity of usher in a school.   There,
his sensitive vanity upon the subject of his
diminutive stature and red hair made him
a butt for boys who were quick to discover
his weak point and merciless in playing
upon it.   He had always been considered
handsome and captivating.   When the lads
ridiculed his fiery locks, and stood on tip-

toe as he passed, to suggest the expediency
of larger growth in a master who assumed
to manage them—he sulked, threw up the
position, and went home.

His next regular situation was that of
tutor in a private gentleman's house, where,
according to his own story, dashed off in
a flashy letter to a friend, his rôle was that
of a masculine Tartuffe, "dressed in black,
and smiling like a saint, or martyr." He
posed as a teetotaller, "a most sober, ab-
stemious, patient, mild-hearted, virtuous,
gentlemanly philosopher, the picture of
good works, the treasure-house of righteous
thought." In this character, he tells of
"drinking tea and talking slander with old
ladies," while "fair-faced, blue-eyed, dark-
haired sweet eighteen" sits admiringly
beside him.

"She little thinks the Devil is so near
her!" subjoins the would-be man-of-pleas-
ure, complacently. The letter from which
the choice excerpt is made winds up, smirk-
ingly, with—"I must talk to some one
prettier, so good night, dear boy!"

His ambition to win laurels as a Love-
lace was patent before his flame-coloured
beard sprouted, and led to serious conse-

quences to other and better people than himself, in after-days.

Portrait-painting—and such portraits !— kept him in pocket- and drink-money for a while. His father partly coerced, partly persuaded him to accept the position which Charlotte, in sheer delight at the prospect of seeing him "steadied down," had described in such vivacious terms to Ellen Nussey—namely, a clerkship on the Leeds and Manchester Railway.

The location was remote from town or village, the salary was small, and the duties were light. The genius had abundant leisure for the cultivation of literary and artistic tastes. Instead of availing himself of it, he sought the acquaintance of neighbouring farmers and manufacturers, partaking of the rude abundance of their tables and, as the shining light in their coarser debauches, "drinking himself violent, when he did not drink himself maudlin."

It goes without saying that he was dismissed for neglect and misconduct after some months of this wretched sort of work.

From Haworth he wrote that his

"recovery from almost *insanity* was retarded by having nothing to listen to except the wind, moaning among old chimneys and older ash-trees,—nothing to look at except heathery hills, walked over when life had all to hope for, and nothing to regret with me,—no one to speak to except crabbed old Greeks and Romans who have been dust the last five thousand years."

He was still at home and still idle when his aunt died, and, during her illness, Mr. Weightman, the curate whose name appears often in Charlotte's and Ellen Nussey's correspondence. "One of my dearest friends," Branwell styles him in a letter to Mr. Grundy, author of *Pictures of the Past*. And of his aunt he adds,—"I have now lost the guide and director of all the happy days connected with my childhood."  -

How fond and firm was his sisters' faith in their only brother is proved, incidentally, by lively messages exchanged, through Charlotte's letters, between him and Ellen a month and more after Miss Branwell's death.

"Branwell wants to know why you carefully exclude all mention of him when you particularly send your regards to every other member of the family. He desires to know whether, or in what, he has offended you, or whether it is considered improper for a young lady to mention the gentlemen of the house."

Charlotte writes this sportively after Ellen's

return to Brookroyd from a visit she paid to Haworth in January, 1843.

In this blindness of devotion is to be found the key to the puzzle of the admiration of his talents and accomplishments felt for him by the more richly endowed members of his family—admiration of which their minds were never disabused.

Miss Robinson hits off his peculiar charm aptly when she says :

"He had a spell for those who heard him speak. There was no subject, moral, intellectual, or philosophic, too remote or too profound for him to measure it at a moment's notice, with the ever-ready fallacious plumb-line of his brilliant vanity. He would talk for hours ; be eloquent, convincing, almost noble ; and afterward accompany his audience to the nearest public-house."

Charlotte left him in the Parsonage when she returned alone to Brussels late in January. The four had had a serenely happy vacation together ; walking on the moors when the weather warranted outdoor excursions ; reading together in the evenings ; exchanging experiences in earnest, or in merry vein. We see them at those Christmas holidays, for the last time, an apparently united and happy household, hopeful for one another, and sanguine in plans for the home-school to be organised at Haworth when the "one year more at the most "— in which M. Héger had predicted that the work of preparation for their chosen profession "would be completed and completed *well*" —had expired.

Then—Charlotte would return from Brussels, bringing diploma and other credentials with her that would ensure a *clientèle* for the seminary ; then—Anne would resign her odious governess-ship ; then — Emily would be such a music-mistress as Yorkshire had never seen.   Perhaps—for fancy grew audacious in building air-castles—the proprieties would not debar Branwell from teaching drawing and painting in a Young Ladies' School conducted by his sisters in his father's house.

The old stone Parsonage would be enlarged with the aunt's legacy, to receive and lodge boarding pupils comfortably, and a few day-scholars might be drawn from the neighbouring farmsteads and the country-houses of mill-owners.

This was the dream nursed by Charlotte in her lonely journey back to Belgium ; by gentle, homesick Anne in turning her face toward a new situation ;  by Emily, joyfully marking out the home-life to be led under the ancient roof-tree by her father, Branwell, and herself, and devising a thousand schemes to unite frugality and dainty variety in her bills-of-fare. Of the three sisters, the boy loved Emily best, and she had most patience with him,—believed that she understood him best of all his kindred. Charlotte had no misgivings for the happiness of either in the first months of her second exile. She could have selected no better guardian for the wayward, brilliant brother than Emily ; no more congenial companion for the eccentric sister than Branwell.

Like most sequels to successful works of whatever kind, Charlotte Brontë's second year in Brussels was a mistake. She was no longer a learner only, but a teacher as well. How repugnant was the task in the circumstances that closed about her upon her return, the reader of *The Professor* and *Villette* may imagine. Emily's absence was a fretting sorrow that made her isolation in the bustling world about her harder to bear.

"M. and Madame Héger are the only two persons in the house for whom I really experience regard and esteem, and of course I cannot be always with them, nor even very often," she writes to Ellen ; and again,— " There is a constant sense of solitude in the midst of numbers. The Protestant, the foreigner, is a solitary being, whether as teacher or pupil."

In the same epistle occurs a warm denial of a rumour which had reached her that "the future *époux* of Mademoiselle Brontë is on the Continent."

" If these charitable people knew the total seclusion of the life I lead,—that I never exchange a word with any other man than M. Héger, and seldom, indeed, with him,—they would, perhaps, cease to suppose any such chimerical and groundless notion had influenced my proceedings."

She laboured assiduously upon the studies that were to qualify her for the principal-ship of the home-school—now the sum of her ambitions. In teaching she was as conscientious as in studying. The term was long—from the first of February to the middle of August ; her fellow-teachers were uncongenial ; her pupils respected, without troubling themselves to love, the alien by birth and faith ; Martha Taylor was dead, Mary Taylor was in New Zealand; the two English families that had opened their houses to her on holidays and Sundays were no longer resident in Brussels, and Madame Héger had conceived a dislike of the outspoken Protestant sub-teacher who scorned to play the spy and regarded the eavesdropper and the pryer into private letters as no better than a thief. What unrecorded passages at arms these two may have had can be guessed at from reading *Villette* and *The Professor*, and the biographies of Charlotte Brontë. While she was an inmate of the Hégers' house Charlotte was honourably reserved as to these encounters.

She is more communicative on this point, as upon others, to Ellen Nussey than to any one else, and the nearest approach to open complaint of her superior that ever crept into her letters to Ellen is discreet, while frank.

The dreary summer vacation passed by her in "the great, deserted Pensionnat, with only one teacher for a companion," and that one a woman without breeding or character,—"a cold, systematic sensualist," —was over. The long, solitary walks, the visits paid, in utter loneliness of heart, to Martha's grave in the foreign cemetery, the footsore wanderings through boulevards

and alleys into the fields beyond the city
limits, with no prospect except other fields,
thinly dotted with trees and outlined by
prim hedges, the wakeful nights, and silent,
appetiteless meals—were exchanged for the
welcome round of prescribed duties.  Upon
one of the many fête-days that relieved the
monotony of work for the other teachers,
she wrote to Ellen :·

" You, living in the country, can hardly believe it is
possible life can be so monotonous in the centre of a
brilliant capital like Brussels, but so it is.  I feel it most
on holidays, when all the girls and teachers go out to
visit, and it sometimes happens that I am left, during
several hours, quite alone, with four great desolate
schoolrooms at my disposition.  I try to read, I try to
write, but in vain.  I then wander from room to room,
but the silence and loneliness of all the house weigh
down one's spirits like lead.

" You will hardly believe that Madame Héger (good,
kind as I have described her) never comes near me on
these occasions.  I own I was astonished the first time
I was left alone thus ; when everybody was enjoying
the pleasures of a fête-day with their friends, and she
knew I was quite by myself, and never took the least
notice of me.  Yet, I understand she praises me very
much to everybody, and says what excellent lessons I
give.  She is not colder to me than she is to the other
teachers, but they are less dependent on her than I am.
They have relations and acquaintances in Brussels.

" You remember the letter she wrote me when I was

in England ?   How kind and affectionate that was !   Is it not odd ?

"In the meantime, the complaints I make at present are a sort of relief which I permit myself.   In all other respects I am well satisfied with my position, and you may say so to people who inquire after me (if any one does).   Write to me, dear, whenever you can.   You do a good deal when you send me a letter, for you comfort a very desolate heart."

It has seemed good, in the temporal *un-fitness* of things, unto certain biographical essayists and sensational penny-a-liners, to deduce, from what Mrs. Gaskell deplores as the "silent estrangement between Madame Héger and Miss Brontë in the second year of her residence in Brussels," the romantic and unsavoury conclusion of a hopeless passion on the part of the English teacher for one of her employers.   This conclusion—bolstered by forced and dishonouring interpretations of passages such as I have just quoted, bearing upon Charlotte's unhappiness in her isolation, her impatience under the limitations of strangerhood and religious prejudices—has been formulated into a theory and dissected, *ad nauseam*, by critics and scandal-lovers on both sides of the Atlantic.   I cannot sufficiently commend the dignified brevity of Mr. Shorter's me-

thod of disposing of a discussion that should
never have been opened.

" Madame Héger and her family, it must be admitted,
have kept this impression afloat. Madame Héger refused to see Mrs. Gaskell when she called upon her in
the Rue d'Isabelle ; and her daughters will tell you that
their father broke off his correspondence with Miss
Brontë because his favourite English pupil showed an
undue extravagance of devotion.    .   .   .

" Now to all this I do not hesitate to give an emphatic
contradiction, a contradiction based upon the only
independent authority available."

After recapitulating the testimony of
Charlotte's surviving schoolfellows—Miss
Lætitia Wheelwright and her sisters—in
support of his refutation of the slander, he
proceeds :

" Madame Héger did, indeed, hate Charlotte Brontë
in her later years. This is not unnatural when we remember how that unfortunate woman has been gibbeted
for all time in the characters of Mlle. Zoraïde Reuter and
Madame Beck. But, in justice to the creator of these
scathing portraits, it may be mentioned that Charlotte
Brontë took every precaution to prevent *Villette* from
obtaining currency in the city which inspired it.   .   .   .
She had received a promise that there should be no
translation, and that the book would never appear in
the French language.   .   .   .   Immediately after her
death the novel appeared in the only tongue understood
by Madame Héger." *

* Shorter's *Charlotte Brontë and Her Circle*, page 109.

To this may be joined the possibility that the original of M. Paul Emmanuel, being an inordinately vain man, even for a Franco-Belgian, was not averse to the reputation of having inspired his most distinguished *élève* with an unconquerable adoration of himself. He corresponded with her after she left school, and she drew much intellectual gratification from his letters, vivacious, stimulating, and sparkling with the caustic wit that made him to be both admired and dreaded in professional and in private life. Charlotte's answers were brilliant essays that might have been read aloud by the Brussels town-crier, yet Madame disapproved so strongly of the association that he instructed Charlotte to address him, for the future, at the Royal Athénée, where he was a professor. The caution was ill-advised; it may have been over-crafty. In the true spirit of a gallant *intrigant*, he may have devised this manœuvre for feeling his way to a fuller understanding with his correspondent, and as a test of her real sentiments to him. If she obeyed the injunction, he was sure of his standing in her affections. The conquest was not important, but it counted for one more upon his list, and it was a novel pleasure to win the first place in the well-kept heart of a demure "English Mees," whose genius he recognised. Aware of his wife's dislike of her late subordinate, and that Charlotte was not ignorant of it, he, as a man of the world, comprehended just what concealment of the exchange of letters from the lynx-eyed *surveillante* signified, and what was implied by mutual confession of the expediency of secrecy. Whatever motive prompted the request, the subtle diplomat was foiled by the single-minded integrity of the country girl.

After *Jane Eyre* had made her famous, she was asked by Miss Wheelwright if she still corresponded with M. Héger. In reply Charlotte stated the simple fact I have alluded to. M. Héger had told her that his wife disapproved of his writing to, or receiving letters from, her, and directed her how to evade her surveillance.

"I stopped writing at once," said Charlotte, in the frank sincerity of innocence. "I would not have dreamed of writing to him when I found it was disagreeable to his wife" — and with calm emphasis,—

"Certainly I would not write unknown to her."

Mr. Shorter's dispassionate conclusion of the whole matter is cordially seconded by all who have had the patience to sift the slander thoroughly, and the candour to repudiate indignantly the tardy attempt to cast a shadow upon the character of a great and a pure woman:

"Let, then, this silly and offensive imputation be now and forever dismissed from the minds of Charlotte Brontë's admirers, if indeed it had ever lodged there."

# CHAPTER XII

SCHEME OF HOME-SCHOOL ABANDONED—BRAN-
WELL'S RETURN HOME—HIS "SHAMEFUL
STORY" AND DOWNWARD COURSE

ON December 19, 1843, Charlotte Brontë wrote to her sister Emily from Brussels :

"I have taken my determination. I hope to be at home the day after New Year's Day. I have told Madame Héger. But in order to come home I shall be obliged to draw on my cash for another £5. I have only £3 at present, and as there are several little things I should like to buy before I leave Brussels—which, you know, cannot be got as well in England—£3 would not suffice. Low spirits have afflicted me much lately, but I hope all will be well when I get home—above all, if I find papa and you and B. and A. well. I am not ill in body. It is only the mind which is a trifle shaken—for want of comfort.

"I shall try to cheer up now.—Good-bye.

"C. B."

The "if I find" had sad significance.

Her sisters had tried to hide from her the knowledge of disasters that were creeping with fatal certainty toward the home that had seemed tranquil and safe a year ago. One of the strongest links in the chain of circumstantial evidence forged by the purveyors of the malodorous scandal treated of in the last chapter is a sentence in one of Charlotte's letters to Miss Nussey of a date subsequent by several years to her departure from Brussels :

"I returned to Brussels after aunt's death, against my conscience, prompted by what then seemed an irresistible impulse. I was punished for my selfish folly by a total withdrawal, for more than two years, of happiness and peace of mind."

The explanation of the remark is as simple as her own uprightness. We have seen how she took upon her young shoulders the elder-sisterly duties laid down at the grave's mouth by Maria, and that the responsibility had never been demitted by her scrupulous conscience. At the death of the aunt who had been the nominal mistress of the house and the guardian of the motherless children, it was borne in strongly upon Charlotte's mind that she ought to forego her dreams of the completed equipment recommended by M. Héger as essential to her success as an instructress, together with her desire to learn German for the sake of the rich literature of that language, and to perfect herself in French and feed her ardent mind with the strong meat it craved. Her place was, she felt, at home. When Emily persisted in her refusal to return to Brussels, asserting her right to remain in the Haworth out of which she was miserable and never well, Charlotte yielded with secret satisfaction for which a conscience, sensitive to morbidness, upbraided her afterward.

For things had gone badly in the Parsonage in her absence. The reason assigned to Madame Héger for what seemed an abrupt resolution to return to England was Mr. Brontë's impending blindness. A cataract was forming upon each eye, and months of darkness and depression must elapse before an operation could be attempted.

This was true as far as it went, but it did not go nearly all the gloomy way. Emily was intensely uneasy at the influence exerted over her father by Mr.

Weightman's successor. The new curate, a rollicking Irishman, richly deserved the castigation he received in *Shirley* as "Peter Augustus Malone." If the whole truth were known, it would be evident, I think, that Mr. Brontë had troubles of his own at this time. He may not have been fond of his sister-in-law when she was alive, but she belonged to his generation, and her years of faithful service in his household gave her a hold upon his heart as upon his gratitude. He missed her sadly, — and Emily was a poor substitute for the woman who had seen in him the true head of the house, the master whose comfort and wishes were to be consulted above everything else in the conduct of affairs. Emily was an excellent housekeeper, and, intellectually, a more congenial companion for her scholarly parent than Miss Branwell. The fact remains that, when Anne had gone back to her post as governess to the daughters of the Reverend Mr. Robinson at Thorp Green, and Branwell had accompanied her as tutor to Mr. Robinson's boys, the Vicar of Haworth was lonely and low in spirits. The curate, with his devil-may-care rattle, diverted his thoughts, and the curate's

REV. PATRICK BRONTÉ

Irish whiskey raised the tone of his nerves. Parson and assistant drank together until the parish whispered ominously of what might be the end of their carousals, and Emily, goaded to desperation by anxiety, took Charlotte into her confidence. Proud, and apparently self-reliant to the rest of the world, she always leaned in spirit upon the elder sister, as upon her arm in their taciturn promenades in the garden behind the Pensionnat in the Rue d'Isabelle.

The shock of the news to Charlotte is inadequately described in her remark to Emily that she is "a trifle shaken." The instant pang of self-reproach in the thought that she might have averted the disaster had she stayed at home, left pain that was slow in departing. The effort to restore her father to his former feelings and habits ; sorrow at his downfall ; the mortification and the nervous strain consequent upon the trial, may well have "robbed her of peace of mind" even before misgivings as to Branwell's behaviour and fate mingled elements of more active bitterness in the cup held to her patient lips.

"I think," she wrote to Ellen Nussey, three weeks after her arrival in England, "however long I may live, I shall never forget what the parting with M. Héger cost me. It grieved me so much to grieve him who has been so true, kind, and disinterested a friend."

He had disapproved so strongly of her resignation of her situation before the curriculum he had indicated was completed, that they nearly quarrelled. "Haworth seems such a lonely, quiet spot, buried away from the world," is a sentence on the same page. "I no longer regard myself as young — indeed I shall soon be twenty-eight, and it seems as if I ought to be working and braving the rough realities of the world as other people do."

The realities were soon to be rough enough, although not of the kind she had coveted. While she and Emily sat together in the parlour, making a set of new shirts for the absent brother, and while tramping the moors,—"to the great damage of our shoes, but, I hope, to the benefit of our health,"—brains and tongue were engaged upon the scheme of the home-school, their one hope of uniting the family and earning a livelihood for themselves and their purblind father.

We will not linger upon the wearisome waiting of the ensuing year (1844). Circulars were prepared and distributed, private letters written to everybody who might be able to forward their plans. The two girls at home, and Anne at Thorp Green, busied themselves with the duties that lay nearest their hands and tried to be patient as the months wore away without a ray of encouragement. Charlotte had resigned all hope of success before the earliest snowdrops bloomed in the Parsonage garden.

"Depend upon it," she wrote to a friend who had interested herself in behalf of the project, "if you were to persuade a mamma to bring her child to Haworth, the aspect of the place would frighten her, and she would probably take the dear girl back with her, *instanter*. We are glad that we have made the attempt, and we will not be cast down because it has not succeeded."

Anne and Branwell were at home for the midsummer holidays. Except that she was paler and quieter than was her former wont, Charlotte saw no alteration in the "little sister." It was a deep delight to pet and nurse her, as in her baby days, and to have her as a third in the walks and talks that were the pleasures of the lonely life in the old grey house it "would have been folly to alter while there was so little likelihood of ever getting pupils." Anne was always satisfactory except as to bodily strength. She rallied, as usual, in the bracing air of the uplands and the atmosphere of home.

Branwell was a disappointment to the whole family and a mystery. Heretofore, the spoiled son of the house had been affectionate and gay-humoured, willing to please others when doing so did not incommode himself, lively in talk, and, as the sisters thought, fascinating in manner. He was now moody and recklessly merry by turns, cross without reason, now boasting of successes he had won, anon berating himself as an ignominious failure, and declaring that he was the victim of remorse, pursued by the furies. Such wild gasconades had never before been heard in the decent dwelling. It was a positive relief to those left behind when he cut short his holiday and hurried back to Thorp Green and work.

At the New Year of 1845 he was again with the puzzled father and sisters. Apparently he was doing better than ever before, holding his tutorship and giving satisfaction to his employers. "He is quieter and less irritable on the whole than he was in summer," is Charlotte's record of the holiday visit. "Anne is, as usual, always good, mild, and patient."

The school project was dead and buried. Not one pupil had applied for admission in response to circulars and private letters. The excitement of preparation and expectation, the alternations of hope and discouragement, the talks of how this room could be cut in two, how a wing could be thrown out from the gable nearest the road, windows enlarged, and others opened—all this was now as dream-like as the busy life at Brussels. Life was a stagnant pool on which mossy scum gathered with the slow passage of time.

In March Charlotte tells Ellen Nussey :

"I can hardly tell you how time gets on at Haworth. There is no event whatever to mark its progress. One day resembles another, and all have heavy, lifeless physiognomies. Sunday, baking-day, and Saturday are the only ones that have any distinctive mark. Meantime, life wears away. I shall soon be thirty ; and I have done nothing yet. Sometimes I get melancholy at the prospect before and behind me. Yet it is wrong and foolish to repine. Undoubtedly, my duty directs me to stay at home for the present. There was a time when Haworth was a very pleasant place to me. It is not so now. I feel as if we were all buried here. I long to travel, to work, to live a life of action."

The dead level was moved from beneath by a new dread. In reading to her almost blind father the reader's own eyes failed her. She fancied that the calamity which had befallen him was about to overtake her. Loss of sight would be a supreme sorrow. In a letter to M. Héger, she confides ambitions of which she had already spoken to Emily and Anne. The ardent mind was tearing away the swaddling-bands of conventionality and diffidence of her native powers. In every pulse and nerve it was quickening and fighting its way toward the air. Formerly she had passed days, weeks —entire months—in writing, she confesses, and not without hope of achieving something worthy in time:

" But at present my eyesight is too weak. If I were to write much I should become blind. This weakness of sight is to me a terrible privation. But for that, do you know what I would do, Monsieur ? I should write a book and dedicate it to my master of literature, the only master that I have ever had—to you, Monsieur ! I have often told you in French how much I respect you, how much I am indebted to your goodness, to your counsels. I could wish to say it once in English. This cannot be. It is not to be thought of. A literary career is closed to me."

How far she was from feeling the resignation she here professes to have attained crops out in other letters.

"Write again soon, for I feel rather fierce, and want stroking down," is the winding up of one.

Her anxiety on her father's account increased daily.

"His sight diminishes weekly. . . . He fears that he will be nothing in his parish. I try to cheer him. Sometimes I succeed temporarily, but no consolation can restore his sight, or atone for the want of it. Still, he is never peevish, never impatient—only anxious and dejected."

Like the bursting of a wind-storm over the ruffled pool was the spectacle that awaited her upon her return from the only visit she allowed herself to make in the sad, tedious summer of 1845. Taking advantage of Anne's arrival at Haworth for the midsummer vacation, Charlotte accepted Ellen Nussey's reiterated invitation to pass a few days with her at Brookroyd. While she was enjoying this breathing spell, Branwell

made an unexpected appearance in his
father's house. Within twenty-four hours
afterwards he had a violent attack of illness,
the effect of a recent debauch.

On the very day of Charlotte's return he
received by mail from Mr. Robinson a stern
dismissal from his tutorship, coupled with
a command never to show his face again
at Thorp Green.

A terrible scene ensued, upon the particulars of which I have no disposition to
dwell. Branwell's story—told a hundred
times to whomsoever would hearken to his
drivellings, and with variations that should
have discounted the authenticity of it—was
that Mrs. Robinson, her husband's junior
by a score of years, had (to quote from his
narrative to his friend and biographer, Mr.
Francis Grundy) "showed him a degree
of kindness which, when he" (Branwell)
"was deeply grieved one day at her husband's conduct, ripened into declarations of
more than ordinary feeling.

"Although she is seventeen years my
senior, all combined to an attachment on
my part, and led to reciprocations which I
had little looked for," is a phrase that brands
the writer as a cad and a puppy, who

would not scruple to sacrifice a woman's reputation to his vanity. The conviction is deepened by the mention in the same recital—or romance—of " the probability of her becoming free to give me herself and her estate."

Mrs. Gaskell believed Branwell's version of the catastrophe, which, he declared to his unhappy death-day, had wrecked his prospects, his ambitions, and his heart. Legal investigation into the shameful story after the publication of the Gaskell biography of Charlotte Brontë proved beyond any reasonable doubt that the intrigue was largely the figment of a brain disordered by drink and opium.

It is within the bounds of probability that Mrs. Robinson may have amused some idle hours by conversation with the versatile tutor who talked so well, and evidently admired her mature beauty. That the affair, which she never thought of as such, ever progressed beyond the initial stage of a pretty woman's enjoyment of a bright young fellow's appreciation of her personal charms, is the most meagre of possibilities.

However fallacious the hopes based upon this good-natured toleration of his devoirs, and however mendacious the tales that outraged the moral perceptions of his relatives, not one of them doubted the substance of the narrative. Mrs. Gaskell had it, with such loathsome details as a virtuous girl, brought up amid puritanical surroundings, could bring herself to repeat. Father and sisters lived and died in the full belief that a false wife and depraved mother was accountable for their darling's ruin. He was so seldom sober after this that he may have wrought his own imagination up (or down) to the pitch of believing his own story.

Ellen Nussey was the one person without the house of mourning who was cognisant of the true state of affairs. She was in feeling, and almost in fact, a daughter of the home so darkly overcast by the misconduct of him who had been almost a brother to her in happier days. To her Charlotte unburdened her heart when the load was insupportable.

On June 17, 1846, we have this record:

"We, I am sorry to say, have been somewhat more harassed than usual lately. The death of Mr. Robinson, which took place about three weeks, or a month ago, served Branwell for a pretext to throw all about him into hubbub and confusion with his emotions, etc. Shortly after came news from all hands that Mr. Robinson had altered his will before he died, and effectually prevented all chance of a marriage between his widow and Branwell ; that she should not have a shilling if she ever ventured to re-open any communication with him. Of course, he then became intolerable. To Papa, he allows rest neither day nor night, and he is continually screwing money out of him, sometimes threatening that he will kill himself if it is withheld from him.

"He says Mrs. Robinson is now insane, that her mind is a complete wreck owing to remorse for her conduct towards Mr. Robinson (whose end, it appears, was hastened by distress of mind) and grief for having lost him " (Branwell). " I do not know how much to believe of what he says, but I fear she is very ill."*

In the first edition of Mrs. Gaskell's *Life of Charlotte Brontë* she relates an incident connected with "the news from all hands," referred to by Charlotte, and which is to this day current gossip in Haworth. The story, in brief, is to the effect that the widow of Mr. Robinson sent a special messenger to inform Branwell of the prohibitory codicil to her husband's will; that, when a summons to meet her envoy at the Black Bull reached the infatuated youth, he dressed himself in his best suit, and "fairly

* *Charlotte Brontë and Her Circle*, page 136.
12

danced down the churchyard," to keep the
appointment. The bearer of Mrs. Robinson's message was closeted with her lover
in the "brown parlour" for half an hour
or so, then came out, mounted his horse,
and went his way.

Much later in the day, some one passing
the closed door of the parlour heard strange,
stertorous breathing, and entering, saw
Branwell Brontë lying on the floor "in a
sort of fit."

It would seem certain that a man from
Thorp Green had an interview with the
late tutor, and brought him unwelcome
news. When we learn from Mr. Shorter's
narrative, that no such clause as was reported by Branwell was attached to Mr.
Robinson's will, which " put no restraint
whatever upon the actions of Mrs. Robinson," furthermore, that Mrs. Gaskell's law-
yer was " fain to confess that his client
advanced certain statements on insufficient
testimony "—we are driven back upon the
persuasion, already expressed, that the
ugly tale owed framework, as well as
colour, to the diseased imagination of a
drunkard and an opium-eater. Something
of his damaging talk had doubtless reached

Mrs. Robinson. Or he may have written to her after her husband's death. In either case, she acted with firmness and propriety in notifying him that there must be no more folly of that kind, and forbidding him to hold any further communication with her. A verbal message was safer than a letter, when she had to deal with such a suitor.

His family and the neighbourhood had nothing but his word for what passed in the "brown parlour." Charlotte, at least, was not in full sympathy with him when she wrote in June, "I do not know how much to believe."

Miss Mary F. Robinson, Emily's biographer, blames Charlotte for her stern reprobation of her fallen brother. When she said to Ellen Nussey that she "could not, and would not, invite her to Haworth while Branwell was at home," that, since she could not say one word, truthfully, in extenuation of his conduct, she would "hold her tongue," she signified that she had cast him out of her heart. His erotic ravings were disgusting ribaldry to her apprehension ; his presence—red-eyed, with bloated sacs above the cheek-bones, and pendulous jaw—was offensive to every instinct of a pure and modest nature. The father might sleep in the room with him to prevent him from blowing out his maddened brains, and Emily sit up into the small hours to "let in the prodigal and lead him in safety to his rest." Charlotte and Anne would be partaker in no man's sins, whatever might be the bond of blood and association. "Anne could only shudder at his sin, and Charlotte was too indignant for pity."

He pitied himself too extravagantly to awaken generous compassion in a stronger nature.

A biographer relates, in illustration of this solace and salve of a weak, diseased conscience, an anecdote of the sister's behaviour to the Castaway, as he loved to call himself. He brought word to her one day that one of the Sunday-school girls was ill and that he had visited her and read a chapter in the Bible and a hymn to her at her request. Charlotte turned upon him a look of wondering incredulity that "wounded him as if some one had struck him a blow in the mouth."

Then, seeming to "accuse herself of having wronged me, she smiled kindly

BRANWELL BRONTË

FROM A DRAWING BY MISS E. TAYLOR

upon me and said, 'She is my little scholar
and I will go and see her.'

"I replied not a word. I was too much
cut up. When she was gone, I came over
here to the 'Black Bull,' and made a night
of it in sheer disgust and desperation. Why
could they not give me some credit when I
was trying to be good?"

Comment is superfluous. Like other
morally infirm people, he cringed and
whined at the lightest lash of retributive
justice. He would have the prodigal's
welcome-feast served ungrudgingly to him
while still in the foreign land and before he
had felt the gnawings of hunger, much less
the pangs of contrition.

He did not need scenes like these to drive
him to the Black Bull. Every penny he
could beg or borrow he spent there, and in
the surreptitious purchase of opium, resort-
ing to the meanest subterfuges to obtain
the deadly drug. More than one attack of
delirium tremens made a hell of the chamber he shared with the brave old blind man.
The brooding quiet of the daintily kept
homestead was broken by maniacal yells
and drunken oaths. The Parson's son and
the pride of the village was a common sot

and hopeless blackguard, and all Yorkshire knew it.

Well might Charlotte write, on the last day of the black and bitter Old Year 1845, to Ellen, who had told her of a similar affliction in another family:

"You say well that no sufferings are so awful as those brought on by dissipation. . . . It seems grievous indeed that those who have not sinned should suffer so largely."

# CHAPTER XIII

STILL-BORN VOLUME OF VERSE—"THE PRO-
FESSOR" REJECTED—OPERATION UPON MR.
BRONTË'S EYES—GREAT SUCCESS OF "JANE
EYRE"—HURRIED TRIP TO LONDON

A LITTLE volume of poems—"a thinner one than was calculated upon," remarked Charlotte in surprised disappointment—was put together by the three sisters in 1845, and timidly offered to a publisher.

By accident, Charlotte had discovered some manuscripts of Emily's which she thought "condensed and terse, vigorous and genuine."

"To my ear," she says, "they had also a peculiar music, wild, melancholy, and elevating."

When, by hours of entreaty and argument, she had "persuaded Emily that such poems merited publication," Anne

"quietly produced some of her own com-
positions. . . .

"I thought that these verses, too, had a
sweet, sincere pathos of their own.  We
had very early cherished the dream of one
day being authors.

"We agreed to arrange a small selection
of our poems, and, if possible, to get them
printed.

"Averse to personal publicity, we veiled
our own names under those of Currer, Ellis,
and Acton Bell."

When to the simple statements made
above are added others to the effect that the
volume was issued at the authors' risk, an
advance of £31, 10s. having been made
by the sisters before it was printed ; finally,
that it fell so nearly still-born from the
press as to merit the title of an utter failure,
—the poor, brief, pitiful tale is told.

In a letter to Thomas De Quincey, accom-
panying a presentation-copy, Charlotte
says, with jauntiness that is a gallant, if
insufficient, mask for an aching heart :

"The consequences predicted have, of course, over-
taken us.  Our book is found to be a drug.  No man
needs it, or heeds it. . . .

"Before transferring the edition to the trunk-makers,

we have decided on distributing as presents a few copies of what we cannot sell."

This was the end of the literary venture that had helped to lift the crushed spirits of the trio above the wreck of the love, the hopes, and the ambitions centred in their hapless brother. While the sisters talked over the enterprise in their nightly promenade of the humble parlour, and Charlotte wrote formal, old-maidish letters signed "C. Bell" to the publishers in London, and one and all concerted economies and sacrifices by which the advance-money could be raised without depleting the family finances—the horror in the house grew more appalling.

"In his present state, it is scarcely possible to stay in the room where he is. What the future has in store I do not know," says Charlotte in March, 1846.

The book of verses stole into, and out of, the literary world in May. In June we hear that "good situations have been offered to Branwell, for which, by a fortnight's work, he could have qualified himself. But he will do nothing except drink and make us all wretched."

In August the oculists pronounced Mr.

Brontë ready to be operated upon for cataract, and Charlotte accompanied him to Manchester for that purpose. The operation was completely successful, the powerful constitution and courage of the venerable patient contributing, in no small measure, to the happy result.

On August 25th, while awaiting the arrival of the surgeon and his instruments, and doing her brave best to keep up her father's spirits for the crucial trial, Charlotte received a small parcel by post. It was the MS. of *The Professor*, a one-volume novel she had written after sending out the poems to try their fortunes among critical publishers. The story was rejected —without thanks—by the firm to which she had submitted it.

The poems—of which I always think as a triple-stemmed lily, springing, straight and stainless, from the mean soil of such new and degrading experiences as had visited the secluded home since the miserable day of the prodigal's unrepentant return—had died in the hour of their birth. By a professional verdict, *The Professor*—the first-fruits of the Brussels life, the harbinger of the unborn *Villette*

—was doomed to a yet more ignominious
fate.

In the fortnight that followed the operation, in the intervals of reading and talking
to her father, as he lay with bandaged
eyes in a darkened room, Charlotte not
only started *The Professor* again upon his
travels from one publishing-house to another, but sat down to write the opening
chapters of *Jane Eyre*. The fructifying bud,
having had a glimpse of day and sunshine,
must and would grow. When once the
story that was to thrill the nations got hold
of her, she knew that she had found her
way into a second and glorious life that
was to be balm and compensation for the
"things that are seen."

The present and temporal demanded all
the fortitude she could summon from every
source. Anne fell ill in the unprecedented
severity of the next winter.

" England might really have taken a slide up into the
Arctic Zone," is Charlotte's mid-December weather report. " The sky looks like ice ; the earth is frozen ;
the wind is as keen as a two-edged blade. . . .
Nothing happens at Haworth ; nothing, at least, of a
pleasant kind. One little incident occurred about a
week ago to sting us to life. . . . It was merely

the arrival of a sheriff's officer on a visit to Branwell, inviting him either to pay his debts, or take a trip to York. Of course his debts had to be paid. It is not agreeable to lose money, time after time, in this way. But where is the use of dwelling on such subjects? It will make him no better."

Mr. Brontë was ill with influenza. Tabby was over seventy, dim of sight, hard of hearing, and hard to please, even by the "children" she idolised. The only water-supply of the Parsonage was from the well at the back, beyond which arose a sloping hillside crowded with graves; the only heat within the stone walls and above the flagged floors came from a starved-looking grate in each "living-room." The cold of the draughty halls bit the flesh and stabbed to the dividing asunder of the joints and marrow. Anne's asthmatic cough was fearfully distressing, often preventing her from lying down at night; Charlotte suffered excruciatingly from toothache, and began to look "grey, old, worn, and sunk," to herself in the mirror.

We know, now, that the weird and wonderful story in which she lived during the few hours she could spare for desk and pen, nerved her to pull through the cruel winter. It was one, and a great one, of the "many, many things she had to be thankful for," when spring, shivering and reluctant, crept up the frozen moorlands. A promised visit from Ellen Nussey was a wholesome stimulant to Charlotte's spent forces. This was to have been paid in May, and after several postponements came to pass in August.

In August, too, *The Professor* knocked, for the sixth time, at a publisher's door. The author was not surprised to receive, a few days thereafter, the MS. that had been submitted to Messrs. Smith & Elder, Cornhill. She *was* pleasurably excited that it was accompanied by a two-page letter of candid, friendly criticism from Mr. W. S. Williams, the professional "reader" of the firm. He had taken the pains to examine the story, and had the sense and taste to discern the merits of it. It was, in his opinion, the work of a person of so much more than mediocre talent that he put himself to the further trouble of writing to "Currer Bell" that, while *The Professor* was not available for the present use of the house, a three-volume novel from the same pen might be. *Jane Eyre* went to London

August 24th, and was accepted as soon as it was read, the second reader to whom the first passed it, sitting up all night to finish it.

In our day of careful typography, triple proof-readings, and elaborate illustration, we catch our breaths in reading that the three-volume novel was "out" in less than a month from the date of acceptance. *Jane Eyre* saw the light, October 16, 1847.

By the opening of the New Year, the public and the critics of both hemispheres were speculating as to the personality of "Currer Bell," and the novel was the "rage" of the literary season.

"I hardly expected that a book by an unknown author could find readers," was Charlotte's modest comment upon her triumph when time had made her reputation sure.

The tremendous venture was known beforehand to nobody except Emily and Anne. The former had sent the MS. of *Wuthering Heights* to a different firm, by whom it was accepted, but without enthusiasm, and published tardily. Anne committed *Agnes Grey* to the same house with a like result. Ellen Nussey heard nothing, in that August visit, of any of the three

books. Each sister had bound herself sol-
emnly to the others not to divulge her
secret without the full concurrence of all
three. The decided aversion to speaking
freely of one's brain-children, especially
when in embryo, natural to authors of fine
sensibilities and true reverence for the gift
that is in them, was almost excessive with
the Brontës—Branwell always excepted.
Even after years of popular favour had
taught Charlotte to hearken to discussions
of characters, situations, and style without
painful embarrassment, it was evident to
her best friends that the subject was delicate and sacred in her esteem. It would
have cost her a hard struggle to take even
trusty and dear Ellen into her confidence
had she been sanguine of success. The
sharp disappointment attendant upon the
former experiment, the recollection of
the fragile lily that had perished with the
blooming, would have closed the lips of
the three most nearly interested in risk and
failure had other reasons for reticence been
lacking.

It was, then, with a strange commingling
of emotions—delicacy, distrust, and exult-
ation—that Charlotte carried a copy of *Jane*

*Eyre*, with a batch of press-notices, into her father's study one afternoon, and, approaching his chair, said, as diffidently as in the days when he set for her the task of an abstract or a composition: "Papa! I've been writing a book."

When he feared her minute handwriting "might try his eyes," if he undertook to read it, she informed him that it was printed. At his ejaculation of dismay over the certain expense and probable failure of an obscure writer, she offered to read some of the reviews aloud, and having allayed his apprehensions somewhat, left book and papers in his hands and slipped away as noiselessly as the shadows to which she was often likened.

Everybody has heard of his sentence of guarded praise, uttered in grim satisfaction fully comprehended by the triad assembled in the parlour at tea-time, fearful of, yet impatient for, his entrance.

"Girls! do you know Charlotte has been writing a book, and it is much better than likely?"

Standing in the parlour, last year, I reproduced to myself, and vividly, the scene, —the plainly laid table, Emily behind the tea-tray; Charlotte seated opposite to Anne, both pale and nervous with suspense, and the tall, gaunt figure of the father, pausing beside the vacant chair at the foot of the board to enunciate the pregnant phrase, a benevolent twinkle in his eyes, a smile he could not suppress hovering about his mobile mouth.

Then, doubtless, the tea was poured and drunk, the bread-and-butter passed, and parish news touched upon, as if nothing uncommon had happened, as if literary circles were not commoved by the apparition of the new star, and every English and American review were not conjecturing, surmising, and affirming as to *Jane Eyre's* creator, whether masculine or feminine, Northerner or Southron, delineator or romancist, and Smith & Elder's mails were not swollen by letters addressed to the mysterious "Currer Bell."

It was impossible that she, being human, should not have derived profound gratification and solemn content from the reward of the travail of her soul and mind. Elated she was not, then or ever. The side of the dual existence she was henceforward to lead with which we have most to do was

13

ballasted by too great and grievous sorrows not to keep within its deeply worn grooves.

Mrs. Gaskell tells us that Charlotte's first thought, when assured of considerable (for her) pecuniary gains from the successful book, was of the "little sister," drooping from too sedentary a life, and bowed to the dust in spirit by the knowledge and sight of Branwell's excesses. As soon as the spring opened, Anne must have change of air at the seashore or elsewhere, strengthening food, such as they could now afford to buy, and the recreations she had missed in her shadowed childhood and girlhood.

But for the inward brightness shed by these hopes, and the intellectual enjoyment of boxes of books forwarded by her publishers, and by her correspondence with Mr. Williams, the routine of home and parish duties was as uneventful and colourless as ever.

Until June ! Then, a letter from Charlotte's publishers broke like a bomb-shell into the little group of student authors. Smith, Elder & Co. had heard, through their American correspondence, that arrangements had been made by a London house for the reprint in the United States of a new book by the author of *Jane Eyre*.   Upon investigation it transpired that the work in question—*Wuthering Heights*—together with *Agnes Grey* and " Acton Bell's " new novel, *The Tenant of Wildfell Hall,* now in press— was believed by the trade to be from the pen of one and the same author, his identity being veiled under three *noms de plume*, Currer, Ellis, and Acton Bell.

In the singleness of their integrity the sisters looked upon the assertion as a slur upon their veracity and honesty.   We smile at, while respecting, the method—to their way of thinking the only way of clearing themselves—chosen and instantly acted upon by the unsophisticated parties under suspicion.   Charlotte and Anne set out for London on the afternoon of the day that brought the agitating letter.   Their trunk was sent a little after noon by a carrier's cart to Keighley, the nearest railway station.   Dressed for the eventful journey, Charlotte and Anne sat down to an early tea, eating little, as we may imagine, and then began the four-mile walk in good season to catch the night train.   A heavy shower wet them to the skin on the road, but they pressed on. Defamation of character was too serious a peril for them to mind trifles when bent upon self-justification.

They went straight from the Chapter Coffee-house (where, odd' as it may seem, they elected to lodge because their father used to put up there as a young man) to Smith & Elder's Cornhill office, amazing the senior partner by presenting the letter he had sent to "Currer Bell." Up to now he and Mr. Williams had written to their author as a man. The publisher turned it over in his hand, and looked bewildered from his own handwriting to the quaint little women standing side by side at the full height of their small stature.

"Where did you get this?" he asked, naturally. Charlotte was spokeswoman, introducing herself as "Currer Bell," her companion as "Acton." In his delight at the solution of more than one vexed question, Mr. Smith would have called together a coterie of literary people at his house to meet the unmasked celebrities, but the visitors would not consent. They would retain their incognita to everybody in London but himself and his partners. After an hour's chat they trudged back to their quaint quarters, never noticing that they were the only women in the house, and Charlotte went to bed with a violent sick headache, the penalty she usually paid for any unwonted excitement.

Mr. Smith so far prevailed over their shyness as to induce them to accompany him and his mother to the Opera that night, where, as Charlotte wrote to Ellen, "fine ladies and gentlemen glanced at us with a slight, graceful superciliousness, quite warranted by the circumstances. Still I felt pleasurably excited, in spite of headache, sickness, and conscious clownishness, and I saw Anne was calm and gentle, which she always is."

The "circumstances" were the plain black silk gowns, long-sleeved and high-necked, made in obsolete fashion by a Haworth dressmaker, and the general air of rusticity that clung to the novices in the gay scene. Charlotte admits the evident provocation of the "graceful superciliousness" without a tinge of false shame. She always rated herself—person and mind—far below the standard set for her by others.

The country girls went to church on Sunday, and afterwards to dine with the hospitable Smiths; on Monday, under their pilotage, to the Royal Academy and the National Gallery; to dinner again at the Smiths', and to tea at Mr. Williams's.

On Tuesday night they were safe at home, wearied out, dazed, and tremulous under the burden of novel experience. "My face looking grey and very old," says Charlotte, "with strange, deep lines ploughed in it. My eyes stared unnaturally. I was weak, and yet restless."

Anne suffered less from the effects of this her first sight of London. Both were content in having accomplished the aim and end of the startling adventure. They had proved to the skeptic the existence of two Bells, and he had accepted their testimony as to the existence of the third. Except to the publishers and their immediate families, they were the "Misses Brown" from Yorkshire. "Shy and reserved little countrywomen, with not much to say," is Mrs. Gaskell's note upon the passing impression they made on such strangers as they chanced to encounter.

Charlotte, as we have seen, "accepted the situation" with, apparently, no thought of the nations praising her near and afar off.

# CHAPTER XIV

## BRANWELL'S DEATH—EMILY'S ILLNESS AND DEATH—A "DREARY CALM"

THE events of the last quarter of the year 1848 will be told here, for the most part, by interweaving extracts from Charlotte's letters into a consecutive narrative. No hand but hers could have sketched them so graphically:

"October 9, 1848.

"The past three weeks have been a dark interval in our humble home. Branwell's constitution had been failing fast all the summer, but still, neither the doctors nor himself thought him so near his end as he was. He was entirely confined to his bed but for one single day, and was in the village two days before his death. He died, after twenty minutes' struggle, on Sunday morning, September 24. He was perfectly conscious 'till the last agony came on. His mind had undergone the peculiar change which frequently precedes death, two days previously; the calm of better feelings filled it; a return of natural affection marked his last moments.

" The remembrance of this strange change now comforts my poor father greatly. I myself, with painful,
mournful joy, heard him praying softly in his dying
moments, and to the last prayer which my father offered
up at his bedside, he added ' Amen ! ' How unusual
that word appeared from his lips you cannot conceive.
Akin to this alteration was that in his feelings towards
his relations. All the bitterness seemed gone.

" He is in God's hands now, and the All-Powerful is
likewise the All-Merciful. A deep conviction that he
rests at last—rests well after his brief, erring, suffering,
feverish life—fills and quiets my mind. The final separation, the spectacle of his pale corpse, gave me more
acute, bitter pain than I could have imagined. Till the
last hour comes, we never know how much we can
forgive, pity, regret, a near relative. All his vices were,
and are, nothing now ; we remember only his woes.

" My poor father naturally thought more of his *only*
son than of his daughters, and much and long as he had
suffered on his account, he cried out for his loss like
David for that of Absalom—' My son ! my son ! ' and
refused to be comforted. And then, when I ought to
have been able to collect my strength and be at hand to
support him, I fell ill with an illness whose approaches I
had felt for some time previously, and of which the crisis
was hastened by the care and trouble of the death scene
—the first I had ever witnessed.

" ' We have hurried our dead out of our sight.' A
lull begins to succeed the tumult of last week. It is not
permitted us to grieve for him who is gone as others
grieve for those they lose. The removal of our only
brother must necessarily be regarded by us rather in the
light of a mercy than a chastisement. Branwell was his
father's and his sisters' pride and hope in boyhood, but

since manhood the case has been otherwise. It has been our lot to see him take a wrong bent ; to hope, expect, wait his return to the right path ; to know the sickness of hope deferred, the dismay of prayer baffled ; to experience despair at last,—and now to behold the sudden, early, obscure close of what might have been a noble career. Nothing remains of him but a memory of errors and sufferings.

" My unhappy brother never knew what his sisters had done in literature. He was not aware that they had ever published a line. We could not tell him of our efforts for fear of causing him too deep a pang of remorse for his own time misspent and talents misapplied. Now, he will never know. I cannot dwell longer on the subject at present. It is too painful." *

To Miss Mary F. Robinson, the enthusiastic biographer of Emily Brontë, we are indebted for other particulars of that last scene of a life that was a confused web of promise and pitiful failure, of folly, and of tragedy :

" He insisted upon getting up. If he had succumbed to the horrors of life he would defy the horrors of extinction. He would die as he thought no one had ever died before,—standing. So, like some ancient Celtic hero, when the last agony began, he rose to his feet. Hushed and awe-stricken, the old father, praying Anne, and loving Emily, looked on. He rose to his feet and died erect, after twenty minutes' struggle."

Charlotte fondly imagined that the suc-

* *Charlotte Brontë and Her Circle*, page 139.

cesses they had been at such pains to hide from him—lest the contrast with the ruin he had made of his own talents and opportunities might add a barb to the remorse she credited him with feeling—never came to his knowledge. His friend and memorialist, Mr. Grundy, reports Branwell as boasting to his boon companions, over their cups, that he had written *Wuthering Heights*, entire or in part, and from another source we have a picture of the braggart, seated in his three-cornered chair in the parlour of the Black Bull, discoursing in tipsy seriousness upon his sisters' achievements and the comparative merits of the three books they had published.

How much of this dishonouring story is true and how much the work of his friends, (!) imaginations, when there was no longer any one alive who could contradict their statements, is not for us to decide. We know the wretched boy to have been a boastful liar where other women's characters were concerned. He was not superior to the meanness of traducing his own flesh and blood, had the opportunity been afforded him. We can only hope, in mercy to his memory, that it was not.

Dismiss we the unspeakably sad and terrible story of the Castaway, in Charlotte's words :

"In GOD's hands we leave him ; He sees not as man sees."

It is an old saying in Yorkshire, as in other parts of England, that when Death enters a house he has not visited in a long time, he leaves the door ajar in going out with his burden. More than twenty years had passed since the pavement of the Haworth Church was disturbed to lay the body of Elizabeth Brontë by her mother and her sister Maria. Looking backward, a shadow falls for us across the page on which Charlotte wrote a week after Branwell's burial :

"Anne is always delicate, and Emily has a cough and cold at present."

The shadow lowers above another entry, dated October 29th :

"I feel much more uneasy about my sister than myself just now. Emily's cold and cough are very obstinate. I fear she has pain in her chest, and I sometimes catch a shortness in her breathing, when she has moved at all quickly. She looks very thin and pale. Her reserved nature occasions me great uneasiness of mind. It is useless to question her ; you get no answers. It is still more useless to recommend remedies. They are never adopted."

Yet more ominous is the bulletin of November 23d :

"I told you Emily was ill in my last letter. She is *very* ill. I believe, if you were to see her, your impression would be that there is no hope. A more hollow, wasted, pallid aspect I have not beheld. The deep, tight cough continues ; the breathing, after the least exertion, is a rapid pant ; and these symptoms are accompanied by pains in the chest and side. Her pulse, the only time she allowed it to be felt, was found to beat 115 per minute. In this state she resolutely refuses to see a doctor. She will give no explanation of her feelings;—she will scarcely allow her feelings to be alluded to. Our position is, and has been for some weeks, exquisitely painful. God only knows how all this is to terminate. I think Emily seems the nearest thing to my heart in the world.

"December 10th.

"Hope and fear fluctuate daily. The pain in her side and chest is better ; the cough, the shortness of breath, the extreme emaciation, continue. As her repugnance to see a medical man continues immutable—as she declares no 'poisoning doctor' shall come near her,—I have written, unknown to her, to an eminent physician in London, giving as minute a statement of her case and symptoms as I could draw up, and requesting an opinion. . . . The crab-cheese arrived safely. Emily has just reminded me to thank you for it. It looks very nice. I wish she were well enough to eat it !"

Emily had not passed the threshold of the Parsonage since she followed her brother's coffin through the dreadful little door in the wall of the churchward front yard, and down the paved walk into the church, where the funeral service was read. Charlotte and Anne had never been robust; Emily had laughed to scorn the thought of physical ailment to her own lithe, active self. She "never minded weather." Wet feet, even a drenching to the skin from a winter storm or a thunder-cloud, were bagatelles. A year before, Anne had written to Ellen Nussey that, while she and Charlotte had suffered much from the prevalent east wind, "Emily considers it a very uninteresting wind, but it does not affect her nervous system." In fact, she denied the existence of a nervous system in her own case.

On the morning of December 19th she lay in bed later than usual, and Charlotte made an excuse for a visit of anxious inquiry—or, rather, inspection, for she dared not ask a question—by taking in to her sister a bit of heather she had been out upon the moors to seek. She had actually found a spray in bloom in a sheltered nook, and displayed it proudly, laying it upon Emily's pillow. Although the cool touch of the pale purple flowers upon her cheek caused the invalid to lift her languid eyelids, she took no notice of them. The lids drooped heavily over the dim eyes, and Charlotte left her, sick of soul and dreading the worst, to make her despairing report to Anne in the parlour. Presently they heard a faint movement in the chamber overhead. Emily was up and, as was her habit, resolutely dressing herself. She sat by the fire, slowly combing her weight of chestnut-brown hair, when the comb caught in the rich masses and fell into the grate. In the extremity of weakness Emily lay back in her chair, panting for breath, and unable to stoop over to recover the comb. Martha, Tabby's young assistant, was attracted from the hall by the smell of burning bone, and Emily appealed to her with a half-laugh,—"My comb is down there ! I am too weak to pick it up !"

Finishing her toilet by slow and painful stages, she wrapped a shawl about her, and holding by the wall to steady her steps, began the descent to the lower floor. Down the crooked stairway, past the well where

her strong young arms had held down and
"punished" poor Keeper—still her devoted
thrall—she staggered, over the cruelly cold
flags of the hall, to the parlour door. Anne
sat by the hearth, her mending basket beside her. Charlotte was writing at the
table in the middle of the room. Both
looked up, but neither ventured to speak
while Emily tottered across the floor to the
hard, straight sofa, and sat down, fitted
her thimble to her clammy finger, and took
up a piece of plain sewing.

The scratching of Charlotte's pen filled
up the brief pauses between the labouring
breaths, each of which was a needle-thrust
in the hearts of the listeners.

This was what Charlotte was saying to
Ellen :

"I should have written to you before, if I had had
one word of hope to say, but I have not. She grows
daily weaker. The physician's opinion was expressed
too obscurely to be of use. He sent some medicine
which she would not take. Moments so dark as these
I have never known. I pray for God's support to us all.
Hitherto He has granted it.

"I hope still, for I *must* hope. She is as dear to me
as life. If I let the faintness of despair reach my heart I
shall become worthless. The attack was, I believe, in
the first place, inflammation of the lungs. It ought to
have been met promptly in time."

The ungenial winter noon saw the abandonment of the poor effort at industry. Emily put aside her work, and lay down upon the sofa.

At her husky whisper Charlotte hastened to her.

"If you—will—send for a—doctor now, I will—see—him !"

Before he could arrive, the last throes were upon her. She grappled with Death as if she were looking into his face, fought breath by breath to wrest her life from his clutch. Her sisters begged her, with tears, to let them get her to bed. Raising herself upon one hand, she motioned them away with the other.

"No ! no !"

Voice, breath, and heart-beat went with the protest. She dropped back upon the sofa, dead—and free !

In six days more, Charlotte sent another letter to her one confidante :

" Emily suffers no more from pain or weakness now. She never will suffer more in this world. She is gone, after a short, hard conflict. She died on Tuesday, the very day I wrote to you. I thought it very possible she might be with us still for weeks, and a few hours afterwards she was in Eternity.

" Yes ! there is no Emily in time or on earth now.

Yesterday we put her poor wasted mortal frame quietly under the church pavement. We are very calm at present. Why should we be otherwise? The anguish of seeing her suffer is over; the spectacle of the pains of death is gone by; the funeral day is past. We feel she is at peace. No need now to tremble for the hard frost and the keen wind. Emily does not feel them. She died in a time of promise. We saw her taken from life in its prime. But it is God's will, and the place where she is gone is better than that she has left.

"God has sustained me in a way that I marvel at, through such agony as I had not conceived." *

"Day by day,"—she wrote three years afterwards,— "when I saw with what a front she met suffering, I looked on her with an anguish of wonder and love. I have seen nothing like it, but, indeed, I have never seen her parallel in anything. Stronger than a man, simpler than a child, her nature stood alone. The awful point was, that, while full of ruth for others, on herself she had no pity; the spirit was inexorable to the flesh; from the trembling hand, the unnerved limbs, the fading eyes, the same service was exacted as they had rendered in health."

Mrs. Gaskell narrates how Keeper, Emily's bulldog ("Tartar") joined the three mourners who walked close behind the coffin as it left the house, followed them into the church, and returned home with them when the service was over. Going directly up-stairs, he stretched his large bulk

* Mrs. Gaskell.

14

across the threshold of his dead mistress's door, and howled mournfully for hours. He visited the place every day for weeks, in evident expectation that the door would open and Emily answer his call. "He never recovered his cheerfulness," says Charlotte.

The Christmas of 1848 was a period of "dreary calm in the midst of which" the human mourners "sought resignation."

" My father and my sister Anne are far from well. As for me, God has hitherto most graciously sustained me. I am not ill ; I can get through daily duties, and do something towards keeping hope and energy alive in our mourning household. My father says to me almost hourly,—" Charlotte, you must bear up ! I shall sink if you fail me.' These words, you can conceive, are a stimulus to nature. The sight, too, of my sister Anne's very still, but deep sorrow wakens in me such fear for her that I cannot falter. Somebody *must* cheer the rest.

" So I will not now ask why Emily was torn from us in the fulness of our attachment ; why her existence now lies like a field of green corn trodden down—like a tree in full bearing struck at the root. I will only say, sweet is rest after labour, and calm after tempest, and repeat again and again that Emily knows that now." *

The first keen anguish of mourning for the lost darling had hardly subsided into the slow torture of missing her, every hour

* *Charlotte Brontë and Her Circle*, page 175.

and minute of lives that must evermore move on without her, when the awful Shade halted for the third time before the door he had left ajar.

# CHAPTER XV

"SLOW DARK MARCH OF THE DAYS"—ANNE'S
DECLINE— HER DEATH AND BURIAL AT
SCARBORO'—CHARLOTTE'S RETURN HOME—
"SHIRLEY"

AGAIN we will let Charlotte's letters take up the sad story:

> "January 10, 1849.
>
> "Anne had a very tolerable day yesterday, and a pretty quiet night, though she did not sleep much. I have just dressed the blister, and she is risen and come down-stairs. She looks somewhat pale and sickly. She has had one dose of the cod-liver oil.
>
> "I am trying to hope, but the day is windy, cloudy, and stormy. My spirits fall, at intervals, very low. Then I look where you counsel me to look,—beyond earthly tempests and sorrows. In the night I awake and long for morning. *Then* my heart is wrung!
>
> "January 15.
>
> "I can scarcely say that Anne is worse, nor can I say she is better. Her cough is most troublesome at

night, but rarely violent.   She is too precious not to be cherished with all the fostering strength I have.

"The days pass in a slow dark march.   The nights are the test,—the sudden wakings from restless sleep, the revived knowledge that one is in her grave, and another, not at my side, but in a separate and a sick bed. However, GOD is over all.

"February 11th.

"Anne continues very much in the same state.   I tremble at the thought of any change to cold wind or frost.   Would that March were well over !   Her mind seems generally serene, and her sufferings are, hitherto, nothing like Emily's.   The thought of what is to come grows more familiar to my mind, but it is a sad, dreary guest."

In March, Ellen Nussey urged affectionately that she might be allowed to accompany Anne to the milder seacoast as soon as the weather grew mild enough for the invalid's removal.   One of the few of Anne Brontë's letters that remain to us was written in acknowledgment of this friendly offer.   After thanking Miss Nussey for her kindness and accepting the proposal,— should she be able to try change of air,— she goes on to speak frankly of the chances of her recovery, weighing them with a calm, collected spirit that enhances our respect for the sweet youngling of the sadly diminished flock.

" I have no horror of death.   If I thought it inevitable I think I could quietly resign myself to the prospect, in the hope that you, dear Miss Ellen, would give as much of your company as you possibly could to Charlotte, and be a sister to her in my stead.

" But I wish it would please GOD to spare me, not only for Papa's and Charlotte's sakes, but because I long to do some good in the world before I leave it.   I have many schemes in my head for future practice—humble and limited, indeed—still I should not like them all to come to nothing, and myself to have lived to so little purpose.   But GOD's will be done ! " *

Charlotte and Ellen took her to Scarboro' on May 24th.   She died there, quietly, on the 28th.   Her last words were : "Take courage, Charlotte ! take courage !"

She was buried at Scarboro', Charlotte and Ellen being the only mourners present.

To her London friend, Mr. Williams, Charlotte wrote on June 25th :

" I am now again at home, where I returned last Thursday.   I call it *home* still, much as London would be called London, if an earthquake should shake its streets to ruins.

" But let me not be ungrateful !   Haworth Parsonage is still a home for me, and not quite a ruined or desolate home either.   Papa is here, and two most affectionate and faithful servants, and two old dogs, in their way as faithful and affectionate.   The ecstasy of these poor animals, when I came in, was something singular.   I am

* Mrs. Gaskell.

certain they thought that, as I was returned, my sisters were not far behind. But here my sisters will come no more. Keeper may visit Emily's little bed-room—as he still does, day by day—and Flossy may look wistfully around for Anne. They will never see them again—nor shall I—at least the human part of me.

" Waking, I think, sleeping, I dream of them ; and I cannot recall them as they were in health. Still they appear to me in sickness and suffering.

" All this bitterness must be tasted. The pain must be undergone. Its poignancy, I trust, will be blunted one day. Ellen would have come back with me, but I would not let her. I knew it would be better to face the desolation at once—later or sooner, the sharp pang must be experienced.

" Labour must be the cure—not sympathy. Labour is the only radical cure for rooted sorrow. The society of a calm, serenely cheerful companion—such as Ellen— soothes pain like a soft opiate ; but I find it does not probe, or heal, the wound. Sharper, more severe means are necessary to make a remedy."

In this persuasion the brave soul gathered up its forces to obey its own prescription. *Shirley* was more than half finished at the time Branwell died. She had not touched the MS. since. The last chapters she had written were read aloud to Emily and Anne, and the future plan of the book was discussed by the three, while pacing the floor in the firelight after ten o'clock at night.

The least sentimental reader must shudder, as at a touch upon a raw surface—or the naked heart—in thinking what the re-opening of desk and portfolio must have been to the desolate mourner in the more than ever quiet house, in reviewing the scenes after writing and reading which she had laid aside her pen. The last chapter read aloud to her audience of two was the twenty-third—" An Evening Out." Anne's gentle praises, and Emily's trenchant, but never unkindly, criticisms, must have annotated each paragraph for her. The heading of the new chapter, not one line of which either of her sisters was ever to hear, was —fitly enough—"The Valley of the Shadow of Death."

The opening passage is too long to be transcribed here. He who peruses it in the recollection of the conditions under which it was penned can discern the trail of life-blood in every line. We trace the same in other portions of this twenty-fourth chapter. It is as if the writer had not yet taken firm hold of her pen, the wand that opened for her the gates to the Wonderland of Imagination, wherein she was to find temporary surcease of pain. Humanly speak-

ing, *Shirley* was her salvation. She
wrought indefatigably upon it all through
the August days, forcing herself to think
of her Other World and the characters with
which she had peopled it, when the song
of the lark floated in at her windows in the
dewy mornings ; as she opened her eyes
upon the square bulk of the church-tower
opposite her window, black against the
flushing sky ; when the blossoming heather
covered "Emily's moors" as with cool
purple mist, and plover and lapwing sang
and whistled in thickets of gorse and bil-
berry. Ellen Nussey entreated that she
might come to Haworth, and share, if she
could not enliven, her friend's solitude.
Charlotte would not consent while the unfinished MS. lay in her desk. "This one
thing I do" was the rule to which she held
herself without complaint or wavering.
She was straitened with the divine com-
pulsion of true genius until it was accomplished.

Not until strait and stress were over did
she speak, even to Ellen, of the desolation
of the evenings when, by the force of
habit, she put up paper and pen at the
stroke of ten, and began pacing the floor

in the old way that used to be sweet, the soft fall of her steps accentuating the stillness that had settled with nightfall in every room. When the wind shook the shrubs under the windows she was thrilled by the fancy of the sweeping garments of viewless visitants stealing up the path to look in upon her loneliness. The cry of an August gale at the closed sashes on one wild, wet night sounded to her like the voices of her sisters, wandering round and round the house, calling inarticulately upon her.

Insomnia and close application to her desk brought on a severe but short attack of illness, just as the last page was written.

"It is gone now," she told Ellen Nussey, thankfully, September 10th. "It is the first from which I have suffered since my return from the seaside."

Upon the same page she makes modest mention of the completed task:

"My piece of work is at last finished, and dispatched to its destination. You must now tell me when there is a chance of your being able to come here."

Before the visit could be paid, there was a minor domestic catastrophe at Haworth. Tabby had a serious fall, just when the

younger servant was ill in bed. Every
housekeeper, even if she be not a literary
worker, will appreciate the sketch Charlotte sent off to Ellen of the general collapse
of her working forces, physical, mental,
and moral :

"I fairly broke down for ten minutes —sat and cried
like a fool. Tabby could neither stand nor walk. Papa
had just been declaring that Martha was in imminent
danger. I was myself depressed with headache and
sickness. That day I hardly knew what to do, or
where to turn.

"Thank Goo ! Martha is now convalescent. Tabby,
I trust, will be better soon. Papa is pretty well. I
have the satisfaction of knowing that my publishers are
delighted with what I sent them. This supports me.
But life is a battle. May we all be enabled to fight it
well ! "

*Shirley*, as every one at all conversant
with modern *belles lettres* knows, was a
superb triumph, and the fidelity of the author's pictures of Yorkshire scenes and
people in a very brief time "ran her to
earth," in sporting phrase. By degrees the
incognita was abandoned. Complimentary
letters rained in upon her from all quarters.
The Smiths induced her to visit them in
London, where she met Thackeray, Miss
Martineau, and a host of lesser literary

lights. She told Mary Taylor, in after-days, that her solitary life had disqualified her for society. "I had become unready, nervous, irritable, excitable, and either incapable of speech, or I talked rapidly. For swarms of people I don't care!"

We have, however, a more pleasing instance of her manner of acquitting herself in her new sphere from an eye-witness of her first meeting with Miss Martineau. The latter was lodging in London, and "Currer Bell" was invited to take afternoon tea with her.

"Miss Brontë was announced, and in came a young looking lady, almost childlike in stature, in a deep mourning dress, neat as a Quaker's, with her beautiful hair smooth and brown, her fine eyes blazing with meaning, and her sensible face indicating a habit of self-control. She came—hesitated a moment at finding four or five people assembled,—then, went straight to Miss Martineau with intuitive recognition, and with the freemasonry of good feeling and gentle breeding, she soon became as one of the family seated around the tea-table."

The delight evinced by her Yorkshire neighbours in the discovery that, as Martha told her young mistress, "Miss Brontë had been and written two books—the grandest books that ever was seen!" touched the

Parson's daughter more nearly than the plaudits of editorial critics. There is a suspicion of tears in the jesting tone in which she informs Ellen that "the Haworth people have been making great fools of themselves about *Shirley.*"

She "valued," too, "more than testimonies from higher sources, a scrap of paper which came into her hands without the knowledge of the writer—a poor working man of this village, a Dissenter. The document is a sort of record of his feelings after reading *Jane Eyre.*"

"On one point do I feel vulnerable," she says to her publishers at the height of her fame. "I should grieve to see my father's peace of mind perturbed on my account; for which reason I keep my author's existence as much as possible out of his way. I have always given him a carefully diluted and modified account of the success of *Jane Eyre,*—just what would please without startling him. The book is not mentioned between us once a month."

Another visit to London was made in 1850. There she had a glimpse of the Duke of Wellington; a morning in the gallery of the House of Commons; an interview with one of her most prominent critics, George Henry Lewes (afterwards the husband of "George Eliot"); calls from titled admirers and learned dignitaries,— and "last, not least, an interview with Mr. Thackeray, who made a morning call, and sat two hours." The London experience was followed by a trip to Scotland, including a stay of a few days in Edinboro'.

"My dear sir," she is moved to tell her publisher, "do not think I blaspheme when I tell you that your great London, as compared to Dun-Edin, is as prose compared to poetry, or as a great, rumbling, rambling, heavy epic compared to a lyric, brief, bright, clear, and vital as a flash of lightning."

In September she was the guest of Sir James and Lady Kay Shuttleworth at their country-seat near Windermere in the Lake Country, and there was introduced to her future friend and biographer, Mrs. Gaskell. To this lady, more than to all other of Charlotte's delineators, we owe our definite impressions of Miss Brontë's *personelle*.

"She is (as she calls herself) *undeveloped*, thin, and more than half a head shorter than I am," Mrs. Gaskell wrote while under the same roof with the famous author. "She has soft, brown hair, not very dark ; eyes, very good and expressive, looking straight and open at you, of the same colour as her hair ; a large mouth ; the forehead square, broad, and rather overhanging. She has a

very sweet voice ; rather hesitates in choosing her expressions, but when chosen they seem without an effort
admirable, and just befitting the occasion. There is
nothing overstrained, but perfectly simple."

From the home-nest at Haworth, always
resought gratefully after the dazzling epi-
sodes we have enumerated, we have a few
lines introductory to a letter to a literary
friend, that " indicate" with true artistic
skill what her life was at this time (1850) :

" Papa and I have just had tea ; he is sitting quietly
in his room, and I in mine ; storms of rain are sweeping
over the garden and church-yard ; as to the moors, they
are hidden in deep fog. Though alone, I am not unhappy. I have a thousand things to be thankful for, and
amongst the rest that this morning I received a letter
from you, and that this evening I have the privilege of
answering it."

In the same September she began, at Mr.
Smith's request, the " sacred duty" of
editing new editions of *Wuthering Heights*
and *Agnes Grey*.

It was reserved for a later generation of
reviewers, represented by Swinburne, Do-
bell, and Matthew Arnold, to do justice to
the genius that produced *Wuthering Heights*.

Charlotte was as nearly resentful as it
was in her nature to be, that Emily went
down to her grave before one note of the

chorus of praise now chanted in her honour reached her ears. Strange as it may appear to us, *Agnes Grey,* a third-rate, colourless story of governess life, fared better with public and critics than Emily's masterly work. We wish, almost passionately, that the surviving sister who strove, while she lived, to win for the dead the honest meed of appreciation, had foreknown the place to be assigned her in forty years' time ; that one of the greatest of nineteenth-century poets would declare that Emily Brontë's soul,

> " Knew no fellow for might,
> Passion, vehemence, grief,
> Daring, since Byron died."

The performance of the "sacred duty" cost the editor dear. "The reading over of papers, the renewal of remembrances, brought back the pang of bereavement and occasioned a depression of spirits well-nigh intolerable."

A timely and pressing invitation to Miss Martineau's was accepted in a sort of sad desperation as soon as the revised books were sent to the publishers. From Ambleside she wrote to Ellen Nussey of the

ELLEN NUSSEY (AT THE AGE OF 65)

FROM A DRAWING BY MISS E. TAYLOR

"temporary relief, at least, by change of air and scene, from the heavy burden of depression which, I confess, has for nearly three months been sinking me to the earth. I shall never forget last autumn ! Some days and nights have been cruel ; but now, having once told you this, I need say no more on the subject. My loathing of solitude grew extreme ; my recollection of my sisters intolerably poignant. . . . I have truly enjoyed my visit here. I have seen a good many people, and all have been so marvellously kind ; not the least so the family of Dr. Arnold. Miss Martineau I relish inexpressibly."

Nevertheless, when in the early spring of 1851 she had a return of what threatened " to crush her with a day-and-night-mare," she would not seek respite or cure from the like means.

" It will not do to get into the habit of running away from home, and thus temporarily evading an oppression, instead of facing, wrestling with, and conquering it— or being conquered by it ! "

The valiant creature would not be conquered any more than she would "run away." She indulged herself, however, with a long visit from Ellen Nussey.

" No new friend, however lofty or profound in intellect, not even Miss Martineau herself, could be to me what Ellen is ; yet she is no more than a conscientious, observant, calm, well-bred Yorkshire girl," she once

15

told Mr. Williams. "She is good ; she is true ; she is faithful, and I love her. Just now I am enjoying the treat of her society, and she makes me indolent and negligent. I am too busy talking to her all day to do anything else."

This sort of busy indolence was good for the morbid soul. The sore heart healed under the influence of such natural, wholesome companionship as other old schoolfellows enjoy who have never drifted apart in place or interests, least of all, in heart and sympathy.

# CHAPTER XVI

MR. JAMES TAYLOR AND HIS REJECTED AD-
DRESSES—VISIT TO ANNE'S GRAVE—"VIL-
LETTE" WRITTEN — ANOTHER NOTABLE
SUCCESS

UPON one subject—newer by far than
'school-day experiences, and of more
imminent importance than literary triumphs
—Charlotte would not be questioned or
bantered by her one intimate friend.

In August, 1849, Smith & Elder had
notified Miss Brontë of their wish to send
a gentleman connected with their house to
Haworth, to receive the valuable manu-
script just completed — *Shirley*. Their
agent, Mr. James Taylor, was Mr. W. S.
Williams's colleague as reader and adviser
for the firm. Charlotte, in reply, offered
"the homely hospitalities of the Parsonage," warning the prospective guest that

he would find "a strange, uncivilised little place," and that his entertainment would be dull, as she had no brother, and her father was too old to "walk on the moors with him, or to show him the neighbourhood." Nothing daunted, Mr. Taylor came, found favour in Mr. Brontë's sight, and proceeded, in a systematic, yet resolute, fashion, to pay his addresses to Mr. Brontë's daughter. He had fared but indifferently well in a twelvemonth, when Charlotte admits to Ellen that "this little Taylor is deficient neither in spirit nor sense," after having assured her that "no matrimonial lot is even remotely offered me which seems to me truly desirable. The least allusion to such a thing is most offensive to Papa."

In this springtime of 1851, just before Ellen came to Haworth, a passage made its way into one of Charlotte's letters that would have encouraged a more timid lover than the quietly persistent man of business, had he read it, or suspected the mood in which it was penned:

"You may laugh as much and as wickedly as you please ; but the fact is, there is a quiet constancy about this, my diminutive and red-haired friend, which adds a foot to his stature, turns his sandy locks dark, and altogether dignifies him in my estimation. However, I am not bothered by much vehement ardour. There is the nicest distance and respect preserved now, which makes matters very comfortable."

Perhaps if Mr. Taylor had been a shade less discreet and cool at this juncture of his wooing, and had pushed the advantage gained by his "quiet constancy," the result would have been different, especially as Mr. Brontë liked him and enjoyed his visits. The news that he was about to quit England for India for an absence of several years had something to do with the sincere analysis of his character and the bias of her estimation in his behalf. He had taken upon himself the selection of the books sent to Haworth regularly from Cornhill. The arrival of the box filled by his thoughtful kindness with food so convenient for her mind that she could not but recognise their intellectual congeniality was the event of the week in her solitude, and kept the little man in hourly and grateful remembrance.

In this favourable state of feeling she prepared for his farewell visit. I think neither Miss Nussey nor herself would have been surprised had he taken his leave as an accepted lover, with a long engagement ahead of him. Charlotte's account of the last interview is so characteristic of her sincere, sensitive nature, and so altogether womanly, that I transcribe it, with a smile of satisfaction:

" Mr. Taylor has been and is gone. Things are just as they were.

" He looks much thinner and older. I saw him very near, and once through my glass. The resemblance to Branwell struck me forcibly. It is marked. He is not ugly, but very peculiar. The lines in his face show an inflexibility and, I must add, a hardness of character which do not attract. As he stood near me ; as he looked at me in his keen way, it was all I could do to stand my ground tranquilly and steadily, and not to recoil as before. It is no use saying anything if I am not candid. I avow, then, that on this occasion, predisposed as I was to regard him very favourably, his manner and his personal presence scarcely pleased me more than at the first interview. . . .

" An absence of five years—a dividing expanse of three oceans—the wide difference between a man's active career and a woman's passive existence—these things are almost equivalent to an eternal separation. But there is another thing which forms a barrier more difficult to pass than any of these. Would Mr. Taylor and I ever suit ? Could I ever feel for him enough love to accept him as a husband ? Friendship—gratitude—esteem I have, but each moment he came near me, and that I could see his eyes fastened on me, my veins ran ice. Now that he is away, I feel far more gently toward him. It is only close by that I grow rigid—stiffening with a strange mixture of apprehension and anger, which nothing softens but his retreat and a perfect subduing of his manner."

She understands herself and the cause of this "repulsion of spheres" more clearly by the time she writes again:

"I am sure he has estimable and sterling qualities, but with every disposition, and with every wish, with every intention, even, to look on him in the most favourable point of view at his last visit, it was impossible to me in my inward heart to think of him as one that might one day be acceptable as a husband. It would sound harsh were I to tell even you of the estimate I felt compelled to form respecting him.

"Dear Nell! I looked for something of the gentleman —something, I mean, of the *natural* gentleman. You know I can dispense with acquired polish, and for looks, I know myself too well to think I have any right to be exacting on that point. I could not find one gleam— I could not see one passing glimpse of true good-breeding. It is hard to say, but it is true. In mind too, 'though clever, he is second-rate—thoroughly second-rate. Were I to marry him my heart would bleed in pain and humiliation. I could not—*could* not look up to him!

"No! if Mr. Taylor be the only husband fate offers to me, single I must always remain. But yet, at times, I grieve for him, and perhaps it is superfluous, for I cannot think he will suffer much. A hard nature, occupation, and change of scene will befriend him." *

* *Charlotte Brontë and Her Circle*, page 317.

As if putting away the subject of this and all other wooings, definitively and with reason, she closes the frank confidence with "I am, dear Nell, your middle-aged friend."

In still another of this most interesting series of letters—unpublished until Mr. Shorter earned our undying gratitude by giving them publicity—Charlotte expresses surprise at her father's attitude towards her admirer. "The least allusion to such a thing is most offensive to Papa," she had said in a preceding epistle. Now, she relates that Mr. Brontë had exhorted the prospective traveller to be true to himself, his country, and God,

"and wished him all good wishes.

"Whenever he has alluded to him since, it has been with significant eulogy. When *I* hinted that he was no gentleman, he seemed out of patience with me for the objection. I believe he thinks a prospective union, deferred for five years, with such a decorous, reliable personage, would be a very proper and advisable affair."

The two parties to the ill-fated love-affair never met again. Mr. Taylor resided in India until his death in 1874, paying several visits to his native land during this

time. In 1863, when Charlotte Brontë
had been eight years in her grave, he married a widow—it is said, not happily.

Mrs. Gaskell pleases us by inserting a
letter so filled with millinery gossip as to
neutralise much she had already said of
Charlotte's indifference to dress. She is
going up to London "in the Season"—
gayer this year than ever before because of
the Great Exposition of 1851—and is be-
comingly and charmingly "exercised" over
a black lace mantle which looked so rusty
over her new black satin that she exchanged
it for "a white mantle of the same price."
She gives the price (£1 14s. 0d.), and
hopes Ellen will not call it "trumpery."
Her heart misgives her that a bonnet bought
in Leeds is "infinitely too gay with its pink
lining." She withstood, on the same day
that she bought the bonnet, some "beautiful silks of pale, sweet colours," and "went
and bought a black silk after all." She
can no more visit Brookroyd before she
goes to London than she can fly, having
quantities of sewing to do, as well as
household matters to arrange. And among
other commissions given to Ellen is one for
"some chemisettes of small size (the full

woman's size don't fit me)—both of simple style, and of good quality for best."

She wore her best raiment a great deal while in London, attending an assembly of the "cream of London society" at Almack's, where Thackeray lectured and singled her out for especial attention before and after the lecture ; where Lord Carlisle introduced himself to her as "a Yorkshireman," and was followed by Monckton Milnes "with the same plea," and where the "cream of society" formed into a double row of staring spectators to gape at the "celebrated authoress" when the lecture was over, and there was nothing for it but to run the gauntlet to the door, with as calm a grace as she could summon at such short notice.

Charlotte sums up her experiences in the great mart in four lines :

"What now chiefly dwells in my memory are Mr. Thackeray's lectures, Mademoiselle Rachel's acting, D'Aubigné's, Melville's, and Maurice's preaching, and the Crystal Palace."

Visits were exchanged between herself and Mrs. Gaskell ; Mr. Williams continued to send her all the new books worth reading, and she wrote clear, crisp critiques of these, when she sent them back ; invitations and compliments rained into her lap with every post ; a visit from her old friend Miss Wooler refreshed her quondam pupil "like good wine" ; at the urgent solicitation of her publishers she began *Villette*, rated by many reviewers as her strongest work—and autumn gloomed into the hard winter of 1851–52. Side by side with talk of great books she was reading, and the great book she was writing, is set this passage :

"Poor old Keeper died last Monday morning, after being ill one night. He went gently to sleep. We laid his old faithful head in the garden. There was something very sad in losing the old dog, yet I am glad he met a natural fate. People kept hinting he ought to be put away, which neither Papa nor I liked to think of."

The wheels of *Villette* "drave heavily" for a while.

"If my health is spared I shall get on with it as fast as is consistent with its being done, if not *well*, yet as well as I can do it. *Not one whit faster!* When the mood leaves me (it has left me now, without vouchsafing so much as a word or a message when it will return) I put by the MS. and wait till it comes back again. God knows I sometimes have to wait long—*very* long, it seems to me.

" However, I can but do my best, and then muffle my head in the mantle of Patience, and sit down at her feet and wait."

When the moors were. greening under warm April showers, and something akin to the glow of health warmed her veins, she confessed to a part of what she had endured in those darksome months :

"I struggled through the winter, and the early part of the spring, often with great difficulty. My friend [Ellen Nussey] stayed with me a few days in the early part of January ; she could not be spared longer. I was better during her visit, but had a relapse soon after she left me, which reduced my strength very much. It cannot be denied that the solitude of my position fearfully aggravated its other evils. Some long, stormy days and nights there were, when I felt such a craving for support and companionship as I cannot express. Sleepless, I lay awake night after night, weak, and unable to occupy myself. I sat in my chair, day after day, the saddest memories my only company.

"It was a time I shall never forget ; but God sent it, and it must have been for the best."

In June, without notifying Ellen of her intention, Charlotte made a solitary pilgrimage to Scarboro', to see for herself whether or not Anne's last resting-place and tomb-stone in the graveyard of the Old Church there were properly cared for. She had given the order to have the memorial slab erected, and what should be inscribed upon it, but had never seen it.   The record is of the simplest :

HERE LIE THE REMAINS OF

ANNE BRONTË

DAUGHTER OF THE REV. P. BRONTË

INCUMBENT OF HAWORTH, YORKSHIRE

*She Died, Aged 28, May 28th, 1849.*

Thus it stands as we see it to-day.   Charlotte found five errors in the lettering and had them corrected, besides having the stone straightened and refaced.   Then she *rested* for three weeks in the very lodging-house where Anne had died three years before, and "was better for her stay."   The sea-air and bathing were a tonic to her nerves, and memories of Anne were soothing, not agitating.   The surviving sister "walked on the sands a good deal and tried not to feel desolate and melancholy."

"How sorely my heart longs for you I need not say," she tells Ellen.   "I am here utterly alone.   Do not be angry.   The step is right. It was a pilgrimage I felt I could only make alone."

She could not at once resume work upon *Villette*.

"The warm weather and a visit to the sea have done me much good physically ; but as yet I have recovered neither elasticity of animal spirits nor flow of the power of composition."

Her father had been a semi-invalid this summer, but shaking off the splenetic humours induced by heat and Haworth drainage, as cooler weather approached, he took note of Charlotte's wan face and languid motions, and insisted that Ellen Nussey be sent for.

The companionship of the deep-hearted, sweet-natured woman, whose tactful sympathy was as invariable as her leal affection, wrought the usual results, although Charlotte had her for but "one little week."

The first instalment of *Villette* went up to London very soon after the gleam of heart-sunshine was shed into the lonely places of the great tender heart, faithful beyond even the faith of woman to the memory of the belovèd dead. In the letter to Mr. Williams announcing the coming of the MS. we get the clue to the miserable inaction of the winter, the spring, and early summer.

> "I can hardly tell you how I hunger to hear some opinion beside my own, and how I have sometimes desponded, and almost despaired, because there was no one to whom to read a line, or of whom to ask a counsel. *Jane Eyre* was not written under such circumstances, nor were two-thirds of *Shirley*."

Like the outflashing of a rainbow against a sombre background of clouds, a sentence springs into view in a note penned immediately after the publication of her third, and what bade fair to be her most famous, book.

"I got a budget of no less than seven papers yesterday and to-day.  The import of all the notices is such as to make my heart swell with gratitude to Him Who takes note both of suffering, and work and motives.  Papa is pleased, too."

# CHAPTER XVII

## MR. NICHOLLS—THE MAN AND HIS WOOING

"PAPA is pleased, too."
The record bears date of February 15, 1853.

There were other things astir in the Parish and Parsonage of Haworth besides the pleasing excitement attendant upon the birth of another successful book—things anent which the Reverend Patrick Brontë was *not* pleased.

In turning back to a letter written by Charlotte to Ellen Nussey, July 10, 1846, we read at the fag-end, and not apropos of the subject-matter of the epistle, a downright contradiction of a rumour alluded to by Ellen to the effect that "Miss Brontë *might* marry her father's curate." Charlotte adds to her denial that the only terms on which she has ever been with Mr. Nicholls is "a cold far-away sort of civility; moreover, that he and his fellow-curates would laugh over the absurdity for six months, if they were to hear of it; furthermore, that they regarded her as an old maid, and that she regarded them, one and all, as highly uninteresting, narrow, and unattractive specimens of the coarser sex."

She is quite as tartly uncomplimentary in October of the next year:

"Mr. Nicholls is not yet returned. I am sorry to say that many of the parishioners express a desire that he should not trouble himself to recross the Channel. This is not the feeling that ought to exist between shepherd and flock. It is not such as poor Mr. Weightman excited." *

Three years had sensibly modified the opinion held by the clergyman's daughter when in the last chapter of *Shirley* she depicted the "unattractive" successor of the whiskey-loving "Malone" as the model curate of the county:

"Decent, decorous, and conscientious, he laboured faithfully in the parish; the schools, both Sunday- and day-schools, flourished under his sway like green bay-trees. Being human, of course he had his faults. These, however, were proper, steady-going, clerical faults. The circumstance of finding himself invited to tea with a dissenter, would unhinge him for a week; the spectacle of a Quaker wearing his hat in the church; the thought

* *Charlotte Brontë and Her Circle*, page 467.

of an unbaptised fellow-creature being interred with Christian rites,—these things could make strange havoc in Mr. Macarthey's physical and mental economy. Otherwise, he was sane and rational, diligent and charitable."

Mr. Nicholls roomed in the sexton's house opposite the churchyard, not a stone's throw from the Rectory. Charlotte describes his keen relish of the novel he would never have read had the author been a stranger, romances not being in his line :

"Mr. Nicholls has finished reading *Shirley*. He is delighted with it. John Brown's wife seriously thought he had gone wrong in the head, as she heard him giving vent to roars of laughter as he sat alone, clapping his hands and stamping on the floor. He *would* read all the scenes about the curates aloud to Papa. He triumphed in his own character."

Which was not surprising, all things being considered. It would appear from this extract that vicar and curate were upon amicable and social terms up to this date (1850), and the lively sense of the ridiculous manifested in the uproar that startled the sexton's wife is further apparent from a reference in one of Charlotte's letters to her father from Filey—near Scarboro', in June, 1852—to the funny proceedings in a di-

minutive old church she had attended on
Sunday :

" At one end is a little gallery for the singers, and
when these personages stood up to perform, they all
turned their backs upon the congregation, and the
congregation turned *their* backs on the pulpit and
parson. Had Mr. Nicholls been there he certainly would
have laughed out." *

She sends kind regards through "dear
Papa" to Mr. Nicholls, Tabby, and Martha,
a classification that implies either disrespect
on the writer's part—an untenable theory
—or a pretty comfortable domestication
of the curate in his superior's household.
Obviously, Mr. Brontë suspected nothing
of what led up to a *dénouement*—and a disagreeable one to him—in the following December. I condense the narrative as given
to Ellen in a long letter from her friend,
enclosing a note from Mr. Nicholls in
answer to one sent by Charlotte after a
conversation with her father.

One Monday evening the curate had
taken tea with the vicar, and Charlotte,
who confesses to having had "dim misgivings" of her own for some time, could
not shake off a certain nervous apprehen-

* *Charlotte Brontë and Her Circle*, page 471.

sion aroused by "his constant looks and strange, feverish restraint." Mr. Brontë had noticed with little sympathy, and much indirect sarcasm, Mr. Nicholls's "low spirits, his threats of expatriation, all his symptoms of impaired health," and it was not singular that the assistant was not tempted to tarry in the study after Charlotte left the two together. Sitting at her sewing in the parlour across the hall, she heard the exchange of good-nights, and "expected the clash of the front door." Instead of this there was a tap at her door, and

" like lightning it flashed upon me what was coming.

"Shaking from head to foot, looking deadly pale, speaking low, vehemently, yet with difficulty, he made me for the first time feel what it costs a man to declare affection where he doubts response."

Delicately as the story is told, we feel, in reading it, that even Ellen would never have been taken so fully into her correspondent's confidence but for Charlotte's solemn belief that she was folding down that leaf of her life forever. She had gone to her father as soon as her suitor left her, and "told him what had taken place."

Mr. Brontë's "agitation and anger" threw

him into a state that menaced apoplexy ;
he raved against the unfortunate lover in
terms that would have been unbearable to
his daughter had her affections been engaged. "As it was," she says, "my blood
boiled with a sense of injustice," although
she promised in haste to dismiss her lover
on the morrow with decision that would
preclude the possibility of a recurrence of
the offence.

She was not unreasonable in explaining
her father's outbreak of ungovernable rage
by referring again to his "vehement an-
tipathy to the bare thought of any one
thinking of me as a wife." In her desire
to pacify him, and the "poignant pity inspired by Mr. Nicholls's state," it slipped
her memory that he was more than willing
to sanction "the little Taylor's " suit.

When the dust of the onslaught upon
the curate, and, incidentally, upon herself,
lifted, she divined the real cause of the first
scene and others that crowded unpleasantly
soon upon it.

"You must understand that a good share of Papa's
anger arises from the idea (not altogether groundless)
that Mr. Nicholls has behaved with disingenuousness in
so long concealing his aim. I am afraid, also, that Papa

246 Charlotte Brontë at Home

thinks a little too much about his want of money. He
says the match would be a degradation; that I should be
throwing myself away ; that he expects me, if I marry
at all, to do very differently ;—in short, his manner of
viewing the subject is, on the whole, far from being one
in which I can sympathise. My own objections arise
from a sense of incongruity and uncongeniality in feelings, tastes, principles."

She concludes by wishing "devoutly
that Papa would resume his tranquillity,
and Mr. Nicholls his beef and pudding,"—
his landlady reporting an utter lack of
appetite.*

If the irate parent had been, instead, the
secret ally of his curate, he could not have
forwarded his interests more surely than by
the course he was pursuing. Mr. Nicholls
would be allowed to retain his curacy only
upon condition that he would never speak
of "the obnoxious subject" again to father
or daughter. Since he would not agree to
this, his days at Haworth were numbered.
The parish took an active interest in the
matter under fire at the Parsonage, and
sided with the vicar. Like him, the parishioners were proud of their celebrity and
ambitious that she should make a brilliant

* *Charlotte Brontë and Her Circle*, page 475.

match, should she ever marry. An old
Haworth resident who saw the wedding,
opened his mind on the subject to me.

"It was not as if she was a common personage, you
see. She was *famous!* If you could have seen the
chariots-and-pairs with liveries that used to roll up this
narrow street and stop at that gate!"—pointing to one
in the wall of the Parsonage garden. "Mr. Brontë pre-
tended to make light of it all, but he had pride in her—
great pride—and he had a right to expect better things
for her than just a country curate—and his own curate
at that. He looked for a rich baronet, at the least, and
he was n't to blame for it."

Mr. Shorter calls our attention to the fact
that Mr. Nicholls, in a spirit of fairness that
does him honour, "always maintained that
Mr. Brontë was perfectly justified in the
attitude he adopted." This judicial and un-
loverly mood was a thing of later growth
than the "temper" which Charlotte regrets
"he showed once or twice in speaking to
Papa"; the "flaysome looks" directed at
Martha, who was "bitter against him," and
that "dark gloom of his," perceptible to
everybody.

Charlotte had excused his depression and
silent endurance of slights and insults :

"They don't understand the nature of

his feelings, but *I* see now what they are," was a floating straw that augured well for a change in the current of her thoughts. " He is one of those who attach themselves to very few ; whose sensations are close and deep, like an underground stream, running strong, but in a narrow channel."

She was never more in sympathy with her truculent parent than when, three months subsequent to this regretful expression, she says, caustically :

"*If* Mr. Nicholls be a good man at bottom it is a sad thing that nature has not given him the faculty to put goodness into a more attractive form. Into the bargain of all the rest he managed to get up a most pertinacious and needless dispute with the Inspector, in listening to which all my old unfavourable impressions revived so strongly I fear my countenance could not but show them."

Mr. Nicholls secured another curacy, yet we see him lingering in Haworth in April of 1853, "sitting drearily in his rooms," except when he went out to walk ; reticent to his brother clergymen ; holding no communication with Mr. Brontë, or with the members of his family, except that he admitted to his room "fat little Flossy," Charlotte's dog, and took him with him in his rambles over the hills. His morose silence and unsocial habits were making him daily more unpopular.

"How much of this he deserves I can't tell," Charlotte writes, perplexedly. "Certainly he never was agreeable or amiable, and is less so now than ever, and, alas! I do not know him well enough to be sure that there is truth and true affection, or only rancour and corroding disappointment at the bottom of his chagrin. In this state of things I must be, and I am, *entirely passive.* I may be losing the purest gem, and to me far the most precious, life can give—genuine attachment—or I may be escaping the yoke of a morose temper. In this doubt conscience will not suffer me to take one step in opposition to Papa's will, blended as that will is with the most bitter and unreasonable opposition. So I just leave the matter where we must leave all important matters."*

The unhappy misunderstanding grew worse in the next month. Mr. Nicholls's evident emotion when he administered the Sacrament for the last time to the people he had served for seven years, drew tears from many eyes and elicited from Mr. Brontë, when it was reported to him, the sneer, "Unmanly driveller!" When pressed by the churchwardens to assign a valid reason for leaving them, he answered that

* *Charlotte Brontë and Her Circle*, page 479.

Mr. Brontë was not in fault. "If anybody was wrong, it was himself, and that the going gave him great pain." Yet, when Mr. Brontë addressed him, "with constrained civility," at a school tea-drinking, the curate was curt to the verge of rudeness, whereat the superior was wroth exceedingly. "I am afraid both are unchristian in their mutual feelings !" sighs poor Charlotte.

The curate was obliged to call at the Parsonage to render into Mr. Brontë's keeping certain parish papers, and Charlotte, seeing him from the window leaning against the gate on his way out, as if spent in strength, or ill, went out to speak to him.

"Poor fellow !" she says. "He wanted such hope and encouragement as I could not give him. Still, I trust he must know now that I am not cruelly blind and indifferent to his constancy and grief. However —he is gone—gone ! and there is an end of it."

It was so far from being the end of it that Mr. Nicholls called at the Parsonage in January of the next year (1854), being on a visit to Mr. Grant, a friendly neighbouring clergyman. Mr. Brontë was stiffly unpleasant, Charlotte so gentle that the call was repeated, and a correspondence begun between her and the self-banished suitor. In March, a note intended for him was slipped, by mistake, into the same envelope with one directed to Ellen Nussey, an accident that led to a full explanation from Charlotte. Ellen was invited to meet Mr. Nicholls at his next visit at Easter. He would stay with Mr. Grant, "as he had done two or three times before, but he would be frequently coming to Haworth."

In April, Charlotte recapitulates the circumstances of the renewal of intercourse. They had corresponded, confidentially, since September of 1853, and the clandestine arrangement weighed so heavily on the daughter's conscience that "sheer pain" made her confess all to her father. There was some "hard and rough work at the time," but the correspondence was not forbidden.

"Mr. Nicholls came in January. He was ten days in the neighbourhood. I saw much of him. I had stipulated with Papa for opportunity to become better acquainted." (After eight years of almost daily association !) "I had it, and all I learned inclined me to esteem and affection. Still, Papa was very, very hostile, bitterly unjust.

" I told Mr. Nicholls the great obstacle that lay in his way. He has persevered. The result of this, his last visit is, that Papa's consent is gained, that his respect, I believe, is won, for Mr. Nicholls has, in all things, proved himself disinterested and forbearing. Certainly, I must respect him, nor can I withhold from him more than mere cool respect. In fact, dear Ellen, I am engaged." *

Mr. Shorter, the first of Charlotte Brontë's biographers to whom were committed the materials for the true story of the stormy courtship detailed in his admirable work, makes short work of the causes that led to Mr. Brontë's grudging consent to the betrothal. I quote the summary:

" Mr. Nicholls's successor did not prove acceptable to Mr. Brontë. He complained again and again, and one day Charlotte turned upon her father, and told him pretty frankly that he was alone to blame—that he had only to let her marry Mr. Nicholls, with whom she corresponded and whom she really loved, and all would be well.

"A little arrangement, the transfer of Mr. Nicholls's successor to a Bradford church, and Mr. Nicholls left his curacy at Kirk-Smeaton, and once more returned to Haworth as an accepted lover."

Charlotte Brontë was now thirty-eight years of age, a year older than her betrothed,

* *Charlotte Brontë and Her Circle*, page 485.

although, on account of her diminutive
stature, small hands and feet, and shy manner, she seemed much younger.

"A tiny, delicate, serious little lady,
pale, with fair, straight hair, and steady
eyes,"—thus Mrs. Ritchie, Thackeray's
daughter, depicts her, when Charlotte—
in whom the company saw "Jane Eyre—
the *great* Jane Eyre"—dined with the
Thackerays. She could hardly reach the
elbow the tall host stooped to offer her,
and at table "sat gazing at him with kin-
dling eyes of interest, lighting up with a
sort of illumination every now and then, as
she answered."

The chosen friend of the intellectual Titan,
fêted by the nobility and bowed down to
by the commonalty, confessed, by wise
and simple, to be the first novelist of her
day, the greatest woman novelist of any
preceding day—she had, deliberately, and in
defiance of opposition from the father she
almost worshipped, engaged to marry
Arthur Bell Nicholls, a poor curate whose
reputation had never gone beyond the
hills that girdled the Haworth valleys. We
may well ponder, word by word, what she
tells her only confidante of her own feel-

ings now that the momentous step was taken.

" For myself, dear Ellen, while thankful to One Who seems to have guided me through much difficulty, much and deep distress and perplexity of mind, I am still very calm, very inexpectant. What I taste of happiness is of the soberest order. I trust to love my husband. I am grateful for his tender love to me. I believe him to be an affectionate, a conscientious, a high-principled man ; and if, with all this, I should yield to regrets that fine talents, congenial tastes and thoughts are not added, it seems to me I should be most presump-tuous and thankless.

" There is a strange, half-sad feeling in making these announcements. The whole thing is something other than imagination paints it beforehand ; cares—fears— come mixed inextricably with hopes." *

As a postscript to this most interesting letter one of her own maxims might be appended :

"I believe it is better to marry *to* love, than to marry *for* love."

What manner of man was he who dared woo a woman of genius, with a soul of fire, and endowed with the divine gift of firing and illumining other souls, the world over ? We ask ourselves the question wonderingly, even after reading what Char-

* *Charlotte Brontë and Her Circle*, page 486.

lotte says of his courage, constancy, and heroic devotion to duty; and even when we have perused Mr. Shorter's eloquent tribute to his valued friend:

> "It is not difficult to understand that Charlotte Brontë had loved him and had fought down parental opposition in his behalf. The qualities of gentleness, sincerity, unaffected piety, and delicacy of mind are his ; and he is beautifully jealous, not only for the fair fame of Currer Bell, but—what she would equally have loved—for her father, who also has had much undue detraction in the years that are past."

In pursuance of my purpose of looking up and cross-examining authorities that have not been made crafty by many interviewers, I went out of my way, upon one of my visits to Haworth, to talk with a man of the people who had been in the parish day-school in Mr. Nicholls's day,— when, as Charlotte says of Mr. Macarthey, "the schools flourished like green bay-trees." My Yorkshireman, beguiled into talkativeness by suggestions, when he would have drawn into his shell if plied with direct interrogations, gave me a portrait that was like a charcoal-sketch in breadth and distinctness :

> "I wor in th' school before and after he married th'

owd Parson's daughter. He wor not, so to speak, a tall man, but of fair height, mebbe five-foot-ten, I should say, an' stocky-like. Broad shoulders, an' a broad face. Sometimes he wore his beard full; sometimes he 'd only whiskers. A master-hand he wor for fresh air. He cut round holes in th' panels of the door of his room at the sexton's where he lodged. Said he could na' get his breath without them. As well as if I 'd seen him yesterday, I moind how he 'd walk in the field back o' the Parsonage every morning after breakfast, rushing up an' down, swinging his arms, an', of a frosty day, beating them across his chest; an' when he 'd kep' this up for half-an-hour or so, an' got himself into a glow, he 'd come tearing down the street and into the schoolroom, where there was only a wee bit of a stove to warm us in the dead of winter, and throw open ivery winder to let in 'real, live air,' he 'd say, pantin' for breath all the time. An'"—laughing and shrugging his burly shoulders in the recollection—"we, poor wee devils, all blue and fair *stairrved* wi' th' cold! He wor niver so friendly in the parish as Mr. Brontë. It wor all work, an' no play, when Mr. Nicholls wor about. Na! not cross, but *harrd* like, an' speaking short an' quick."

From other sources, among them Charlotte's admissions, before his indomitable devotion and her father's injustice moved her to pity, and pity to "esteem and affection"—we gain the same idea of a lack of personal magnetism in the man she married. How far physical robustness and muscular energy appealed to one always

REV. ARTHUR BELL NICHOLLS

FROM A DRAWING BY MISS E. TAYLOR

fragile, and seldom really well, we may suspect, but cannot determine. She was pitiably lonely. Fame had brought her hosts of acquaintances and a few true friends, without enriching home loves or supplying domestic companionship. She loved her father almost with passion, in the absence of anybody else to love. She was never intimate with him at any time, and with advancing years his liking for solitude, when once within the Parsonage walls, increased. Oftener than otherwise, his only child took her meals alone in the parlour, haunted for her by a host of torturing memories. In the evening she sat, solitary, there, unless when Ellen Nussey was her guest.

An argument which certainly had great weight with the dutiful daughter was Mr. Nicholls's voluntary pledge (kept religiously until Mr. Brontë's death in 1861) that he would be "support and consolation to her father's declining years." Her letters show how poignant was her alarm at any and every illness that attacked the old man, and how abject the sense of her helplessness when these were likely to be serious. A sentence in one of the half-dozen letters

17

written after her marriage is pregnant with meaning, taken in this connection:

"Each time I see Mr. Nicholls put on gown or surplice, I feel comforted to think that this marriage has secured Papa good aid in his old age."

If we wish, in reading it, that a mistress of nervous, pertinent English had used some other word than "comforted," we take refuge in Mr. Shorter's assertion—and no more trustworthy evidence could be adduced—"that the months of her married life, prior to her last illness, were the happiest she was destined to know."

# CHAPTER XVIII

MARRIAGE—MARRIED LIFE—ILLNESS AND DEATH

"CHARLOTTE BRONTË'S trousseau was bought at Leeds." The sentence recurs to the memory of each member of the "Brontë Cult," in passing through the busy, unromantic city. She planned what gowns she should buy, and how they should be fashioned, in the course of a three days' visit to Mrs. Gaskell in May. The wedding was to take place June 29. She consulted her hostess, also, as to certain inexpensive alterations to be made in the Parsonage.

A small room back of the parlour, used, heretofore, for domestic stores—flour, coals, etc.,—was paved with coarse flagstones; the walls were rough-cast. Charlotte would have a board floor laid upon the cold stones, although, if this were done, there would be

an awkward step up from the hall. Mr.
Nicholls's one besetting physical ailment
was a rheumatic tendency, and no carpet
Charlotte could afford to buy, or that would
be congruous with the other appointments
of the Parsonage, would prevent the chill
of the flags from striking through to his
feet. The new boards were to be covered
with a green-and-white ingrain of good
quality; the walls would be hung with a
green-and-white paper, and the one window
with curtains to match.

The two distinguished women had more
to say of domestic economies and decora-
tion in those three days than of books, and
publishers, and fame. Holy Nature is justified of her children when these are women.

The bride-expectant wrote complacently
to her friend, on her return to Haworth, of
the "little new room." The green-and-
white curtains were up ; they exactly suited
the papering, and "looked clean and neat
enough." To Ellen she fears that dear
old Miss Wooler, one of the few persons to
be invited to the wedding, may think her
former pupil negligent because she had not
written sooner.

"I am only busy and bothered. I want

to clear up my needlework a little, and
have been sewing against time since I was
at Brookroyd. Mr. Nicholls hindered me a
full week."

Which naïve statement " comforts " us
in no small measure, as being more like
" lovering " talk than anything else she has
said.

Miss Wooler and Ellen Nussey arrived
quietly at the Parsonage on the 28th of
June. After the three friends had had tea,
and discussed in full the arrangements for
the morrow, they sat long together in the
purple twilight, talking tenderly of the past,
hopefully of the future, Mr. Brontë remaining, as was his custom, in the study. Not
until Charlotte went in to bid him " Good-
night " did he inform her that he did not
intend to be present at the marriage. He
would stay at home while the ceremony
was performed. Remonstrance and petition were in vain. He was calmly stub-
born in his refusal, and the dismayed trio,
retreating to the parlour, consulted the Ru-
bric for a possible way out of the dilemma.
The injunction that the bride shall be received by the officiating clergyman " from
her father's or *friend's* hand " furnished

an expedient. Miss Wooler would give away the daughter whose natural guardian had deserted her at the eleventh hour.

Mrs. Newsome (Sarah De Garrs) puts in a plea for Mr. Brontë's conduct on this occasion, which it is but fair to read :

"I think I understand his absenting himself from the church. There are many of us who feel heart-break at the marriage of ' our own,' even 'though all seems well. In his case it was pathetic. The Brontës had been a family where a joy must be shared by each member, or lose its flavour. The father would seem to see each dear absent face as they individually presented themselves to his mind's eye, and he could not trust himself. Charlotte understood her father, while Miss Wooler could only see the proprieties."

Whatever weight may be attached to the apology, it is creditable to the framer's heart, and may temper our indignation in the thought of the little band of three women who next morning slipped silently out of the gate opening into the side-street, and walked the fifty yards or so lying between gate and church-porch. Mr. Nicholls, the clerk, and the clergyman awaited them there. The ceremony, brief as it was, gave time for the circulation of the astounding news that "Miss Brontë, dressed like a bride," had gone into the church with Mr. Nicholls. When the party emerged from the lobby, the steps were filled by open-eyed spectators. Among them were three people who told me of the scene.

The bridal dress was of worked muslin ; a pretty lace mantle was worn over it. The pure white "chip" bonnet had a wreath of green ivy-leaves about the crown. Mrs. Gaskell compares the wearer to a "snowdrop." Those who saw her say that she looked absurdly small and young—"quite like a little girl just from her first communion."

The wedding-breakfast was served and waited upon by Martha Brown, and she helped the bride change the white muslin for the travelling dress. We saw this in the Brontë Museum at Haworth,—a glacé silk, of a warm dove colour, with a narrow white stripe in it, and trimmed with a sort of brocaded galloon. Her bonnet was of "drawn" or "shirred" silk ; her shawl—also preserved in the Museum—is in colour between drab and grey, all wool and soft in texture. This was her Sunday costume for the rest of that season, except when she varied it by substituting for the woollen shawl one of white taffeta—also on exhibition among the Brontë relics.

The collection, I may mention here, comprises other mementos infinitely touching to the tender-hearted visitor as indicative of the frugal simplicity of a life that ran parallel with the brilliant literary career, without being deflected by a hair's breadth from its even tenor, or catching more than fleeting glints of light from it. Besides the execrable portraits executed by the artist brother, there are pencil-sketches wrought with painstaking minuteness by Charlotte when she, too, dreamed of expressing her genius with brush and crayon. Criticism is disarmed by the recollection. Samplers, worked by the mother and each of her daughters ; the MS. of *The Professor*, almost unreadable to the naked eye, but clear as copperplate under a glass; Charlotte's expense-books, in even smaller script, yet perfect in every letter and figure ; Keeper's collar—perhaps the same in which Emily knotted her strong fingers in dragging him down the stairs; a brooch, enclosing a lock of Charlotte's soft brown hair; a jet necklace which was one of her scanty store of ornaments; collar and cuffs,

home-made, of Brussels net and lace, that
were hers; a fragment of the black-and-
white print gown she gave to Martha
Brown to wear to the wedding, and a
pink print figured with white—a house-
gown of her own, made by herself as a
part of her trousseau—each has a tale to
tell, and all are of Charlotte Brontë at Home
—not of the eminent novelist.

Currer Bell lives for us no longer when
the wheels of the carriage—with white
"favours" at the horses' ears, and the
same upon the coachman's breast—rumble
down the long steep street. Henceforth,
it is Mr. Nicholls's wife whom we see—
the "Charlotte" known and tenderly cherished by, at most, four or five people of
the hundreds who had met and talked with
her.

This Charlotte it was who dispatched a
short note to Ellen from Conway, the first
stage of the wedding-journey. It had been
"pleasant enough thus far"; the evening
was "wet and wild, 'though the day was
fair chiefly, with some gleams of sunshine."
Ellen must let her know by return mail
"how she and Miss Wooler got home.

"On Monday, I think, we cross the

Channel." Her husband was Scotch by parentage, but Irish by birth, and the vacation was spent in Ireland.

The bride "liked her new relations." "My dear husband, too, appears in a new light in his own country"—is a pleasing paragraph in a home letter.

" More than once I have had deep pleasure in hearing his praises on all sides. Some of the old servants and followers of the family tell me I am a most fortunate person, for that I have got one of the best gentlemen in the country. I trust I feel thankful to GOD for having enabled me to make what seems a right choice, and I pray to be enabled to repay, as I ought, the affectionate devotion of a truthful, honourable man."

The same note is sounded in a communication to Ellen Nussey, shortly after they were resettled at Haworth. At a school tea-drinking, celebrating the home-coming of the wedded pair, a parishioner proposed Mr. Nicholls's health as a "consistent Christian and a kind gentleman." Tame praise this in our ears, considering the occasion, yet the newly wedded wife was "deeply touched by the thought that to merit and win such a character was better than to earn either wealth, or fame, or power. I am disposed to echo that high, but simple eulogium."

In a graver vein—not free from sadness —she imparts to her friend some views she has adopted in the month and a half that divide her from the wedding-day :

" Dear Nell ! during the last six weeks the colour of my thoughts is a good deal changed. I know more of the realities of life than I once did. I think many false ideas are propagated, perhaps unintentionally. I think those married women who indiscriminately urge their acquaintance to marry, much to blame. For my part, I can only say with deeper sincerity and fuller significance what I always said in theory,—' Wait God's will.' Indeed, indeed, Nell, it is a solemn and strange and perilous thing for a woman to become a wife. Man's lot is far, far different." *

The invitation to pay her a visit at the earliest opportunity, urged in this letter, is reiterated in another written in September. Charlotte grudged the splendid weather when her friend did not come on the appointed day. "The moors are in glory. I never saw them fuller of purple bloom." (As she was never to see them again !)

Mr. Nicholls flourishes in health, "having gained twelve pounds in Ireland."

* *Charlotte Brontë and Her Circle*, page 493.

Then, "Arthur" slips from the tip of the
pen, and the lapse is prettily apologised
for : "It has grown natural to me to use it
now."

Ellen must get away from an invasion
of visitors at Brookroyd, and come to
Haworth, where she was impatiently expected—a petition granted in October.

In November — "Arthur wishes you
would burn my letters. It is not 'old
friends' he mistrusts, he says, but the
chances of war—the accidental passing of
letters into hands and under eyes for which
they were not written."

She and Arthur contemplate a visit to
Brookroyd, and it is again alluded to as a
probability later in the month. Sir James
Kay Shuttleworth and a friend have been
guests at the Parsonage from Saturday until after dinner on Monday, and the mistress
of the manse has been kept very busy with
her guests.

An oft-postponed meeting of the two
friends was again deferred by Arthur's
dread lest his wife should contract a fever
then prevalent in the Brookroyd neighbourhood. Arthur, it is evident, had taken all
her business into his capable hands. She

quotes him three times in a note of fourteen lines, and begins one dated December
7, 1854, with the half-regretful, half-
jesting—

"I shall not get leave to go to Brookroyd before
Christmas, now, so do not expect me.  Arthur is sorry
to disappoint both you and me, but it is his fixed wish
that a few weeks should be allowed yet to elapse before
we meet.  Probably he is confirmed in this desire by
my having a cold at present.  I did not achieve the walk
to the waterfall with impunity.  Though I changed my
wet things immediately on returning home, yet I felt a
chill afterwards, and the same night had sore throat and
cold ; however, I am better now, but not quite well.

"Did I tell you that our poor little Flossy is dead?
He drooped for a single day and died quietly in the night
without pain."

She can hardly understand why she is
busier than ever before, "but the fact is,
whenever Arthur is in I must have occupations in which he can share, or which will
not, at least, divert my attention from him."
Her Christmas letter to Brookroyd in-
cludes Arthur's holiday greetings with hers.
" He is well, thank God ! and so am I, and
he is 'my dear boy,'— certainly dearer
now than he was six months ago.  In three
days we shall actually have been married
that length of time ! "

The wedded pair visited the Kay-Shuttle-worths in January, and our hearts, quite melted by the spontaneity of the "dear boy" phrase, stiffen and cool when January 19 comes, and excuses are still made for their non-appearance at Brookroyd. The wife "hopes to write with certainty and fix Wednesday, the 31st of January as the day, but——"

The "but" is to us a black cloud settling down between those who had loved so faithfully through so many and such chequered years. Charlotte's own health is now the obstacle to going anywhere. She hints at a possible and natural cause for the "indigestion and continual faint sickness" that have been her portion for ten days. Her friend must keep the matter wholly to herself while it is so uncertain.

"I am rather mortified to lose my good looks as I am doing just when I thought of going to Brookroyd."*

The November excursion to the "Brontë waterfall" was "dear Arthur's" idea. Charlotte was just sitting down to her desk to write a letter when he summoned her to a walk. They had tramped half a mile

* *Charlotte Brontë and Her Circle*, page 499.

before he suggested the waterfall. It would be swollen by melting snows and worth seeing. Of course Charlotte instantly reminded herself how often she had "wished to see it in its winter power," and the tramp was extended over two miles farther. While they were watching the "torrent racing over the rocks, white and beautiful," it began to rain, and they "walked home under a streaming sky.

"However, I enjoyed the walk inexpressibly, and would not have missed the spectacle on any account."

As we have seen, the loyal, valiant little wife took a heavy cold, attended by a sore throat and cough that wore upon her strength. While at Gawthorpe, the seat of the Kay-Shuttleworths, she added to her cold by another long walk. The ground was wet and cold, and we are amazed at learning that her own prudence and Arthur's zealous care of her health did not prevent her from wearing thin shoes on the expedition. Sore throat and cough were abated somewhat, but not entirely gone, nor had she recovered the strength they had wasted, when the "perpetual nausea and ever-recurring faintness"—pronounced to be hopefully symptomatic by the medical man whom Mr. Nicholls summoned—overtook her. She had been confined to her bed for some weeks—too weak and exhausted to keep her feet any longer even to wait upon her husband—when the first of two pencilled notes was sent to Ellen Nussey :

"I must write one line out of my dreary bed. I am not going to talk of my sufferings. It would be useless and painful. I want to give you an assurance which I know will comfort you—and that is, I find in my husband the tenderest nurse, the kindest support, the best earthly comfort that ever woman had. His patience never fails, and it is tried by sad days and broken nights. Papa—thank God ! is better. Our poor old Tabby is *dead and buried !*"

Tabby had died suddenly, and although her great age and often infirmities had made her more of a care than a help for several years past, her death was a shock and a sorrow to the one survivor of the four children she had tended with motherly devotion. Martha Brown was Charlotte's efficient nurse. Mrs. Gaskell recounts how she tried from time to time to cheer her with the thought of the baby that was coming. "I daresay I shall be glad sometime," she would say. "But I am so ill ! so weary !"

She put her hand—now so wasted that
the light struck through it when she lifted
it—to paper about the middle of February,
1855. The letter was to the Miss Wheelwright who had been her schoolmate in
Brussels :

"A few lines of acknowledgment your letter *shall*
have, whether well or ill. At present I am confined to
my bed with illness, and have been for three weeks. Up
to this period since my marriage I have had excellent
health. My husband and I live at home with my father.
Of course I could not leave *him*. He is pretty well,
better than last summer.

"No kinder, better husband than mine, it seems to
me, there can be in the world. I do not want now for
kind companionship in health, and the tenderest nursing
in sickness.

"Deeply I sympathise in all you tell me about Dr.
W. and your excellent mother's anxiety. I trust he will
not risk another operation. I cannot write more now;
for I am reduced and weak. GOD bless you all !

"Yours affectionately,
"C. B. NICHOLLS."

The unfailing courtesy and kindly con-
sideration for others' welfare that had
proved her a thoroughbred in health were
with her still; her filial piety and unselfish
fealty to her husband were strong in
death, as in life. For the two in whom

18

her constant soul was bound up she struggled with death hourly at closer quarters.

Mr. Shorter has rounded off her correspondence as it should be, if there be any
truth in "the eternal fitness of things,"
with the hitherto unpublished last letter
Charlotte Brontë wrote,—and it was to
Ellen Nussey :

"Thank you very much for Mrs. Hewitt's sensible,
clear letter. Thank her, too. In much her case was
wonderfully like mine, but I am reduced to greater weakness. The skeleton emaciation is the same. I cannot
talk. Even to my dear, patient, constant Arthur, I can
say but few words at once.

"These last two days I have been somewhat better,
and have taken some beef-tea, a spoonful of wine-and-
water, and a mouthful of pudding at different times.

"Dear Ellen ! I realise full well what you have gone
through, and will have to go through with poor Mercy "
(Ellen's sister). "Oh, may you continue to be supported
and not sink. Sickness here has been terribly rife.
Kindest regards to Mr. and Mrs. Clapham, your mother,
—Mercy. Write when you can.

"Yours,

"C. B. NICHOLLS."

"The relentless nausea and faintness,
still borne in patient trust," never relaxed
their hold until the end was sure. February
had gone, and half of March, when the

fluttering pulse quickened with fever; her mind wandered; she was thirsty and faint. Could something be given to make her stronger? Beef-tea, brandy, milk, were tried in turn. The stomach could retain nothing. She sank steadily, sleeping most of the time, from utter exhaustion, and speaking but once in her last night on earth.

Her husband, kneeling by her bedside, and praying for the precious passing life, saw the beautiful eyes open upon his. They were full of wistful love, the lips were parted in a whisper :

"I am not going to die—am I? *He* will not separate us! We have been *so* happy !"

She drew her last breath early on the morning of March 31, 1855.

A testimonial to Charlotte Brontë, exquisite in diction and full of feeling, was written by Mr. Thackeray for the *Cornhill Magazine* in April, 1860. It accompanied two chapters—all that were penned—of the last story ever begun by the author of *Jane Eyre*. The unfinished tale is headed EMMA. Nothing she ever wrote surpasses the fragment in crispness and pathos. The heroine is a lonely child, supposed for a while to be an heiress, discovered in the second

chapter to be deserted, penniless, friend-
less—the victim of a cruel impostor.

Mr. Thackeray throws open the door of
the Parsonage parlour for us, to reveal a
tableau for which we must ever bless him.
It is a home idyl, at the sight of which a
distrustful, resentful pain we have tried to
ignore, even to ourselves, leaves our hearts.
A new and softer light plays over the figures of the husband and wife. We can
thank GOD, with her, that loneliness and
lack of sympathy are things of the past.
She had acknowledged to Ellen that
"Arthur's" bent was wholly towards matters of life and active usefulness, "little inclined to the literary and contemplative."
He was, nevertheless, an interested listener,
a cordial sympathiser, and a gentle critic of
her work.

This is Mr. Thackeray's sketch :

"One evening, at the close of 1854, as Charlotte
Nicholls sat with her husband by the fire, listening to
the howling of the wind about the house, she suddenly
said to her husband, 'If you had not been with me, I
must have been writing now ! '

"She then ran up-stairs, and brought down and read
aloud the beginning of a new tale. When she had finished, her husband remarked, 'The critics will accuse
you of repetition.'

"She replied, ' Oh ! I shall alter that.   I always begin two or three times before I can please myself.'

" But it was not to be.   The trembling little hand was
to write no more.   The heart, newly awakened to love
and happiness, and throbbing with maternal hope, was
soon to cease to beat ; that intrepid outspeaker and
champion of truth, that eager, impetuous redresser of
wrong, was to be called out of the world's fight and
struggle."

Charlotte Nicholls made her will February
17th, two days after she wrote to Miss
Wheelwright.   Although "much reduced
and very weak," her mind was perfectly
clear, and we have no reason to think that
she then doubted her final recovery.   As a
proof that she did not, a clause bequeaths
to her husband the interest of her property
during his lifetime—"in case I leave issue";
in which event the principal was to revert
to her "child or children."   Should she die
without issue, everything was left unre-
servedly to him.   He was sole executor.
Her father and Martha Brown were the
witnesses.   Mr. Nicholls took out letters of
administration April 18, 1855.

For six years he remained an inmate of
Haworth Parsonage, Mr. Brontë's assistant
in church and parish, his affectionate son
at home.   Regarding his wife's father as a

sacred trust from her, he fulfilled it will-
ingly, patiently, even tenderly — until the
old man fell asleep after a tedious illness,
June 7, 1861, aged eighty-four years.

Mr. Nicholls then returned to Ireland,
where he still lives, beloved and respected
by a large circle of friends, held by his immediate relatives to be "the best of men."
After his removal to his native land he married a second time.  His wife was Miss
Bell, a cousin ; and Mr. Shorter gives us the
assurance that the union " has been one of
unmixed blessedness."

# CHAPTER XIX

### THE HAWORTH OF TO-DAY

FORTY-ONE years after the great novelist and true woman had laid down
the insupportable burden of mortality, I
went on my first visit to Haworth.

In many perusals of works that are to
me still miracles of creative genius, when
I recall the peculiarly secluded life of the
writer and the circumstances under which
they were produced, Charlotte Brontë had
come closer to my heart than many of my
living friends. The most commonplace
description of her appearance or habits, the
most meagre detail of her personal history
had fascination for me that did not abate as
mature years brought disillusion to many
other dreams. My approach to the scenes
among which she had lived, laboured, suffered, and died, was as to a shrine.

The Haworth railway station is situated between the new factory village of that name, built upon the hill to the traveller's left as he alights from the London train, and upon steeper hills on the right. Over and between these last twists a foot-path, passing two or three black stone cottages and farm-buildings, and bringing up abruptly at what is surely the steepest street ever laid out by a sane surveyor. It is paved with flat stones set edgewise, to afford hoofs a possible "purchase"; shops and cottages, all built of the blackened stone one sees everywhere here, and roofed with slates, line the way to the top of the hill, where stand the rectory and the church. At the very gate of the latter is the ancient hostelry, the Black Bull. The landlord, whose father and grandfather kept it before him, apologises for the "new" and modern front, which is but fifty-odd years old. The staircase of solid stone is worn into deep ruts by the tread of a dozen generations of long-lived Yorkshire folk.

By the time we had taken possession of the comfortable bedrooms and parlour assigned to us, and ordered " a genuine Yorkshire tea," twilight was settling upon the valleys; but we sallied forth, impatient for a first glimpse of the Parsonage. The wing, added to it under circumstances of which I shall speak presently, leaves the original building intact as to exterior. We knew it at a glance, from the many pictures as familiar to us as any scenes in our own country. It is an oblong stone house of two stories, with two windows on each side of the front door, and a row of five windows above, with a chimney topped with tiles, or "pots," at each end. A stone pediment projects over the door, besides which there is nothing to relieve the bare ugliness of the frontage. The churchyard slopes away from it down to the church and village. At the beholder's left it also slopes directly down to the gable, in which is set a solitary window, and shuddering conjectures as to drainage and water-supply force themselves upon the least practical. The burial-ground is literally paved with weather-and-smoke-blackened tombstones. There is not so much as a footpath between them.

"The back part of the house is extremely ancient," says Charlotte in *Shirley*. "It is said that the out-kitchens there were once enclosed in the churchyard, and there are graves under them."

The family at the Parsonage had no neighbours of their own rank. On the farther hills are the residences of prosperous mill-owners and country gentry, but the Brontës had no means of reaching them except on foot. No carriage of any kind was to be had in Haworth.

Within this cramping shell of circumstances, contracted sometimes with the rigour of the thumb-screw, glowed and throbbed genius that compelled the admiration of all English-reading peoples. The lives these girls led in and for and of themselves were as far removed from, and as unlike, the world of their actual environment as the tropics from the arctic pole.

Leaning against the square tower which is all that remains of the old church, while the night mists gradually blotted out the grim outlines of the rectory, we spoke musingly of these things, and marvelled the more in silence.

Whence did the sisters draw their inspiration? Where in experiences, confined almost entirely to the wild Yorkshire parish and the dull routine of a Brussels boarding-school, did they find even the suggestions of Rochester, and Blanche Ingram, of Robert Moore and Catherine Linton, of Mr. Sympson and Dr. John? What in these waste lands kept alive the holy fires of imagination, and nourished fancy, and held back from despair natures so dissimilar to those of their daily associates that the very tongue in which they wrote and spoke was like a foreign language?

A slow rain drove us by-and-by to the shelter of our inn. Our evening meal, excellent in quality and abundant to profusion, was served in a parlour adorned with photographs of the old church and rectory, and warmed by the dancing flames of a soft-coal fire. A window of my bedroom looked upon the churchyard; the rear wall of the church was not twenty feet away.

The rising wind, blowing down from the moors, drove the rain in intermittent streams against the parlour windows, as we mused before the fire and dipped into *Jane Eyre*, *Shirley*, and *Villette* to steep our souls yet more thoroughly in "local colour." The scrape and tramp of hobnailed shoes upon the stone floor of the pass-

age without our door helped the illusion
that set dates at naught. The tap-room
company was assembling for a Saturday
evening sitting and smoking and decent
quaffing of the famous Black Bull brew.
It was easy to imagine that "th' Parson's
son" would presently be sent for; impossible not to strain our ears to catch the
sound of his quick run down the steep
street, his bound through the paved entry,
the roar of applause that welcomed him.
Those of our party who visited the tap-
room brought back more tales of him—the
village demigod and the family disgrace—
than of father or sisters.

Sunday morning dawned brilliantly clear.
As soon as breakfast was dispatched, we
set out for a stroll over the moors—Emily's
even more than Charlotte's moors, although
the foot-path, gained by a turnstile at the
side of the rectory wall, leading through
several fields to the wide commons, and
over them to the "Brontë" waterfall,
bears the name of "Charlotte Brontë's
favourite walk."

The sweep of the air over the hills billowing against the horizon on every side
of us was the elixir of life. Look where

we might, we saw hills! hills! hills!—blue
in the hollows, black in the gorges, green
upon brow and sides with the short, thick
turf that grows nowhere else as in this sea-
girt, fog-draped island, and criss-crossed
by the stone walls separating one freehold
from another. Cattle were grazing in these
fields; upon hillsides and hilltops we could
discern here a cottage, there a spacious
farmstead, and we counted four church-
towers within a radius of perhaps twenty
miles; but the region is sparsely settled
outside of the mill towns, and except in
the ravines there are so few trees that the
effect of generous spaces in summer and
of bleak nakedness in winter can never be
absent from the view.

In the springtime the miles of moorland
are dappled green; "some of the fields are
pearled with daisies, and some golden with
king-cups"; in August the meads take on
a deeper green, and the moors are royal in
purple raiment. Mrs. Gaskell describes
them, when the bloom had been beaten off
by a thunder-storm, as of a "livid brown."
When we saw them, the heather, darkened
by frost, was almost black when crossed
by a cloud; the slopes of wild grass were

bleached to a pallid yellow. To the listeners upon the serene heights that glorious Sunday morning, with only a world of purest air betwixt them and heaven, were wafted across the valley notes of one church-bell after another, until the ether was vibrant with celestial melody.

Flocks of low-flying swallows skimmed the pale grasses, and hardy robins ran fearlessly before us as we descended. We saw but one human creature besides ourselves in a walk of an hour and a half.

Before entering upon a description of Haworth church and rectory, I feel constrained by a sense of justice to correct, so far as is in my power, the popular prejudice with regard to the changes made in both of these buildings since the death of Mr. Brontë left the living vacant. The duty to set down as briefly as is consistent with accuracy the history of these alterations is the more binding upon my conscience because I had, prior to my visit to Haworth, joined in the strictures passed upon what, to the distant admirers of the matchless sisters, was little short of sacrilege.

At the time of Mr. Brontë's decease the

Parsonage was well-nigh uninhabitable, the church almost a ruin. Haworth was scourged periodically by low and typhoid fevers, and at length an official analysis of the drinking-water of the village revealed truths so revolting that the authorities in charge of public affairs insisted upon bringing in a purer and more abundant supply from a distance. Mr. Brontë refused to have it introduced into the Parsonage. The well in the yard, from which he and his children had drunk for almost twoscore years, was good enough for him.

The Parsonage was ill-ventilated, damp, and cold; the windows were few and small, having been put in when the tax upon glass burdened householders.

Poverty, seclusion, drudgery, climatic severity, and repeated bereavements would have tamed the young eagles into the meekest of barn-yard fowls had the genius that animated them been less than miraculous in fervour and might. They had meat that their associates knew not of.

Outside of the Parsonage the *un*sanitary conditions were yet more appalling. The churchyard teemed with the dead, and fresh interments were made almost daily.

"Family graves," unknown in America except among the foreign population, were filled to within a few inches of the surface. The tiny dooryard separating the Parsonage from the cemetery was lower than the swollen level on the other side of the fence, and when the wind blew over the burial-ground into the front windows it brought pestilential gases into sleeping- and living-rooms.

The church stood farther down the slope, and in wet weather foul pools oozed up between the stone slabs of the floor. This lay by now over a foot below the graves pressing upon the outer walls. The deep digging of the "family grave" had under-mined the foundations ; the rear wall bulged and cracked, and the galleries "sagged" from the loosened stones of the interior. On the streetward side outhouses and other nuisances had been set close against the windows. So objectionable was the church as a place of worship that the better class of parishioners would not attend divine service here, and the congregation dimin-ished steadily, although the population of the district was increasing rapidly.

Mr. Brontë's successor, the Rev. Mr.

Wade, a man of energy, scholarship, and refinement, in making public the report of experts to the effect that the Haworth church was unsafe, and would have to be rebuilt from the foundations upward, made application by letter to hundreds of wealthy and influential people who had left their names in the visitors' book kept at the Parsonage. Selecting what seemed to him promising addresses, he wrote out a plain statement of the dilemma in which he found himself, and asked for funds with which to restore the sacred edifice as nearly as was practicable to the original form, using the old stones in the erection. The only donation received for this purpose was one of thirty pounds from an opulent nobleman. Meanwhile he was met by a demand from his own parish for a more commodious house of worship. Since the ruin must come down, it was better, reasoned sensible and interested parties, to provide suitably for the needs of a growing parish, already too large to be accommodated within the bounds of the ancient sanctuary. When the plans of such a church were laid before the people they raised all the money required for its construction, one man head-

ing the subscription list with five thousand
pounds.

The tottering walls were levelled to the
ground, the heaving pavement of the floor
was lifted. Under the chancel had been
interred the remains of the family that had
lent distinction to the obscure hamlet. The
dust of father, mother, and six children was
mingling with the common earth, Mr.
Brontë's coffin being scarcely six inches
underground. The honoured relics were
removed reverently, under Mr. Wade's personal direction, and placed in a vault
constructed upon the same spot, and her-
metically sealed. A brass plate let into the
floor of the new church designated the
place.

These are incidents unknown to non-
residents of Haworth, and sorely perverted
in the course of the newspaper controversy
provoked by the intelligence of the demoli-
tion of the "Brontës' church." Criticism
yet more caustic followed the addition of
the new wing to the rectory, a dwelling
altogether insufficient in size for the family
that had removed into it. Nobody cares to
recollect, if anybody has troubled himself
to listen to the simple statement, that before

enlarging the dwelling the new incumbent proposed to sell it, instead, to the clamouring protestants, that the Brontë relics (then to be had by the score) might be therein collected and preserved. To employ his own words, he "was called to this parish to conserve the highest interests of the church committed to him, and not to act as the curator of a museum." If the Brontë admirers would buy the old Parsonage he would erect a new one elsewhere. His proposal met with no response, except in the form of sentimental protests against the profanation of a shrine. Nobody raised any objection to his planting the churchyard with trees, which have thriven upon the mouldering mortality beneath.

These are not pleasant details, but I do not apologise for giving them ; I could not say less. Nevertheless, I gladly pass on to the less gruesome features of my story.

The inability to appreciate the actuality of present environment on the part of one who has sought a shrine in the character of "the passionate pilgrim," is a misfortune common to sensitive tourists. A notable exception in my own experience in this respect was the sensation that thrilled me almost to pain in crossing the worn door-step where Charlotte must have sat or stood times without number to see the sun set and the moon rise, the teeming grave-yard, overrun with nettles and long grass, stretching between her and the dark square tower of the church.

As Emily had trod beside us on our moorland tramp, so the elder sister whom the world knows so much better seemed to glide to my side and accompany me through the house her genius had con-secrated.

We were taken, first, into the room at the right of the entrance, once Mr. Brontë's study—or den—where he used to hear the children's lessons, and Branwell's Latin and Greek ; where he read *Jane Eyre* on the critical afternoon of its presentation to him by the author ; where he bullied his would-be son-in-law out of reach of patience and politeness ; where he sat when refusing to give his daughter "in marriage to this man."

It is bright now with sunlight which the windows have been enlarged to admit, paper of a soft neutral tint conceals the rough walls, books fill the shelves, and pictures are set and hung here and there. It looks like what it is—the workroom of a thoughtful scholar of liberal views and refined tastes. Yet I could not get away from the unuttered fancy that a chill had been left in the air by the old man when he dropped, like a dead leaf, into his shallow grave under the church pavement.

Across the hall is the room in which "the girls" wrote *Jane Eyre, Wuthering Heights, Shirley, The Tenant of Wildfell Hall,* and *Villette,* the little volume of verse published tentatively by the trio, and the many verses written and never printed. This was the family sitting-room,—the "parlour,"—in which meals were served, and where the sisters wrote, sewed, studied, and received their few visitors. It is of fair size, and, as furnished now, pleasant and cozy. When scantily fitted up with such articles as were positively needed for carrying on the daily routine of domestic life and occupations, bare as to walls and floor, and insufficiently heated by the small grate, it must have owed whatever it had of cheer and comfort to the fact that it represented to the inmates home, and liberty to follow the pursuits they loved best.

From the children's fireless "study," often spoken of in our former chapters, we passed into the "girls' room" adjoining, gazing there, with bowed heads and full hearts, upon the spot where stood the "dreary bed" of Charlotte's next-to-the-last letter to faithful Ellen Nussey.

At a subsequent visit we were admitted to the heart of the Parsonage-home as it now is,—a large, cheery, handsome library-parlour in the wing. At our first call, we saw none of the Rector's family except himself. Under his care we returned to the church, where we had already attended service that morning. The brass tablet above the sealed grave under the chancel, the gift of a stranger-admirer, is lettered, *Emily and Charlotte Brontë*. What would the "brilliant" only son have said and felt could he have foreseen the omission of his name from the family roll of honour? A fine stained-glass window, inscribed, "*To the glory of God, and in pleasant memory of Charlotte Brontë,*" was placed in the new church "by an American citizen," whose identity is a secret to all but Mr. Wade,— a secret he has preserved inviolate. Tablets commemorative of the rest of the Brontë

household interred within the sanctuary are
let into the wall near the door.

In the lobby we were shown the marriage register of Arthur Bell Nicholls and
Charlotte Brontë.   Until Mr. Wade inter-
fered to protect it by locking up the precious volume in the safe, of which he keeps
the key, the record was seen and handled
by every sight-seer, and as a result Charlotte's signature, the last she penned of her
maiden name, is shockingly bethumbed
and soiled.   Both parties to the contract
are said in the register to be "of full age";
Mr. Nicholls's father is written down "a
farmer," Mr. Brontë as "clerk."

I bought a photograph of Mr. Nicholls
from a Haworth man whose shop is hard
by the church.   The face had a decided
Milesian cast, and, to my disappointed eyes,
wore a smug, pragmatical look.

"It is a fairish likeness," the "old resident" assured me.   "He is an Irishman,
you know, and is still living—near Dublin,
I think.   *Hers* is a better likeness," desig-
nating the picture we have learned to know
by heart, the thin, shy face, redeemed from
absolute plainness by the glorious eyes.
"Recollect her?   I've lived here, as man

and boy, all my life, and seen her thousands of times. I saw her married. None
of us ever dreamed that any of them would
come to be famous, unless it was the son.
He was the cleverest lad I ever knew, and
the best company in the world. He could
have been anything he chose if he had conducted himself differently. We were surprised that *she* became distinguished, she
was so quiet and reserved. The old Parson
had some queer ways with him. He always slept with his pistols by him, and
they were never far away from him. A
few days before he died he was handling
one, and found his finger was too weak to
pull back the trigger. So I, being handy
that way, was sent for to make a lever that
would work it. As a family they kept very
much to themselves ; but if it had n't been
for them, Haworth would never have been
heard of. Mrs. Brown, the old servant
' Martha,' who lived so long with them,
died several years ago."

Mr. Wade's disinclination to receive
within the rectory the throng of sight-seers
who troop thither from all parts of the
world has been the subject of animadver-
sion as virulent as that called forth by the

alterations in church and parsonage. When one pauses to reflect that the annual visitation used to be numbered by thousands, and still mounts up into the hundreds, that the Rector is a busy man and a studious, conscientious in the discharge of parochial and domestic duties, and that even a clergyman is supposed to have some of the rights of a private citizen to hold his home as his castle, the present incumbent of Haworth may be less bitterly censured for declining to grant the run of his premises to the curious and the sentimental public.

For ourselves, we frankly owned that exclusion, even of reverent pilgrims, ought not to be construed into discourtesy ; and the knowledge of his scruples and general practice in this respect made us appreciate the more gratefully the hospitable invitation to visit the sacred precincts.

We said our grateful farewells to him upon the hollowed threshold of his front door—the gray, old stone sill which, by some occult process, brought the "tiny, delicate, serious little lady, pale, with fair, straight hair and steady eyes," to our spiritual vision more vividly than anything else about the house had done,—and bent our steps thoughtfully back to the Black Bull.

In the warm noon sunshine, a robin was singing in the laurestinus and golden-holly trees fringing the sunny side of the church ; above, the sky was blue and smiling as a baby's eyes ; out on the moors the wind blew fresh and strong ; the swallows flew low, and in sheltered hollows the late-blossoming heather looked fearlessly up to Heaven.

# INDEX

London, 93, 95, 105, 133, 134, 219, 233, 234, 280
" Lowood," 51, 55

## M

" Macarthy, Mr.," 242, 255
" Malone, Mr.," 128, 166, 241
Martineau, Miss Harriet, 219, 220, 224, 225
Milnes, Monckton, 234
" Moore, Robert," 283
Morgan, Mrs., 11
Morgan, Rev. William, 8, 11

## N

Nelson, Lord, 4
Newsome, Mrs., iv, 18, 262
Nicholls, Arthur Bell, 240–253, 255–258, 260–263, 265–
    272, 277, 278, 295
Nussey, Ellen, 74, 75, 77–79, 84–86, 88, 95, 105–107,
    115, 118, 119, 121, 123, 130, 133, 139, 150, 151,
    155, 156, 164, 167, 171, 173, 176, 179, 182, 189,
    190, 197, 205, 207, 213–215, 217, 218, 224, 225,
    229, 236, 238, 240, 243, 244, 251, 254, 257, 260,
    261, 265–268, 272, 274, 294
Nussey, Henry, 120, 122, 127, 129
Nusseys, The, 116

## O

O'Prunty, 3

## P

Penzance, 4, 21, 82, 148
*Professor, The*, 135, 136, 154, 156. 186, 187, 189, 264

# BELLES-LETTRES

## Little Journeys

**to the** Homes **of Good** Men **and Great**
**to the** Homes **of American Authors**
**to the** Homes **of Famous Women**
**to the** Homes **of American Statesmen**
**to the** Homes **of Eminent** Painters

Fully illustrated. 16°, each, $1.75; per set, $8.75.

## The Ayrshire Homes and Haunts of Burns

By HENRY C. SHELLEY. With 26 full-page illustrations from photographs by the author, and with
portrait in photogravure. 2d edition. 16°, $1.25.

"This is one of the pleasantest and least controversial of the
recent contributions to the literature of Burns. . . . A very
interesting, useful, and attractive book."—*London Spectator.*

## Lyrics and Ballads of Heine

Goethe, and Other German Poets. Translated by
FRANCES HELLMAN. Second edition, revised and
enlarged. 16°, $1.50.

"An exquisitely made little book is the second edition of
the Lyrics and Ballads of Heine. The translations are happy,
smooth, and flowing, and with no little vigor."—*New York
Evangelist.*

## The Complete Works of Washington Irving

NEW KNICKERBOCKER EDITION. Forty volumes,
printed on vellum deckel-edged paper from new
electrotype plates, with photogravure and other
illustrations. 16°, gilt tops, each, $1.25.

G. P. PUTNAM'S SONS, NEW YORK AND LONDON

# Historic Towns of New England

Edited by LYMAN P. POWELL. With introduction by GEORGE P. MORRIS. With 160 illustrations. 8°, $3.50.

## CONTENTS:

Portland, by S. T. PICKARD; Rutland, by EDWIN D. MEAD; Salem, by GEORGE D. LATIMER; Boston, by T. W. HIGGINSON and E. E. HALE; Cambridge, by S. A. ELIOT; Concord, by F. B. SANBORN; Plymouth, by ELLEN WATSON; Cape Cod Towns, by KATHARINE LEE BATES; Deerfield, by GEORGE SHELDON; Newport, by SUSAN COOLIDGE; Providence, by WM. B. WEEDEN; Hartford, by MARY K. TALCOTT; New Haven, by F. H. COGSWELL.

# Historic Towns of the Middle States

Edited by LYMAN P. POWELL. With introduction by ALBERT SHAW. With 160 illustrations. 8°, $3.50.

## CONTENTS:

Albany, by W. W. BATTERSHALL; Saratoga, by ELLEN H. WALWORTH; Schenectady, by JUDSON S. LANDON; Newburgh, by ADELAIDE SKEEL; Tarrytown, by H. W. MABIE; Brooklyn, by HARRINGTON PUTNAM; New York, by J. B. GILDER; Buffalo, by ROLAND B. MAHANY; Pittsburgh, by S. H. CHURCH; Philadelphia, by TALCOTT WILLIAMS; Princeton, by W. M. SLOANE; Wilmington, by E. N. VALLANDIGHAM.

# Some Colonial Homesteads

And Their Stories. By MARION HARLAND. With 86 illustrations. 8°, $3.00.

"A notable book, dealing with early American days. . . . The name of the author is a guarantee not only of the greatest possible accuracy as to facts, but of attractive treatment of themes absorbingly interesting in themselves, . . . the book is of rare elegance in paper, typography, and binding."—*Rochester Democrat-Chronicle.*

# More Colonial Homesteads

And Their Stories. By MARION HARLAND. Fully illustrated. 8°, $3.00.

# Where Ghosts Walk

The Haunts of Familiar Characters in History and Literature. By MARION HARLAND, author of "Some Colonial Homesteads," etc. With 33 illustrations. 8°, $2.50.

"In this volume fascinating pictures are thrown upon the screen so rapidly that we have not time to have done with our admiration for one before the next one is encountered. . . . Long-forgotten heroes live once more; we recall the honored dead to life again, and the imagination runs riot. Travel of this kind does not weary. It fascinates."—*New York Times.*

G. P. PUTNAM'S SONS, NEW YORK AND LONDON

www.ingramcontent.com/pod-product-compliance
Lightning Source LLC
Chambersburg PA
CBHW021755110726
47902CB00006B/1532